FIELDS OF HOME

FIELDS OF HOME

Marita Conlon-McKenna

Illustrated by Donald Teskey

Holiday House / New York

DEDICATION

For my husband, James, with love

Text copyright © 1996 by Marita Conlon-McKenna
Illustrations copyright © 1996 by The O'Brien Press Ltd.
ALL RIGHTS RESERVED.

Originally published by The O'Brien Press Ltd., Ireland
First published in the United States by Holiday House, Inc. 1997
Printed in the United States of America

Library of Congress Cataloging-in-Publication Data
Conlon-McKenna, Marita.
Fields of home / by Marita Conlon-McKenna ; with drawings by
Donald Teskey.
p.   cm.
Summary: In latter part of the nineteenth century, their varied
circumstances in Ireland and in America convince Peggy and Michael
O'Driscoll and Eily O'Driscoll Powers of the importance of family.
ISBN 0-8234-1295-4
[1. Family life—Ireland—Fiction.   2. Ireland—
History—1837–1901—Fiction.]   I. Teskey, Donald, ill.   II. Title.
PZ7.C761845F1   1997   96-39132   CIP   AC
[Fic]—dc21

Contents

CHAPTER 1

The Homestead

MARY-BRIGID WALKED ACROSS the tufts of springy summer grass, helping her mother, Eily, to carry the heavy
washbasket. She loved days like this when the sky was
so blue and the grass so green you could almost hear
it grow beneath your feet.

She could see her Daddy, John, down below in the
potato field, weeding the drills. This year there would
be a grand crop, he'd said, to judge by the healthy
green leaves and stalks – and that's what all the men
were saying. Bella, the milking cow, moved slowly
through the field beyond the potato patch, chewing
constantly and flicking away the annoying flies with
her tail.

'Mary-Brigid, will you pass me up that shift and those

stockings of Nano's?' called Eily.

Mary-Brigid lifted up the soaking garments to her mother, giggling as water from the clothes dripped down her bare, skinny legs and onto her feet, drenching the bottom of her loose, blue cotton dress. Soon the line of rope that stretched between the young oak tree at the end of the field and the wooden pole near the house was bedecked with an assortment of wet clothing. Finally, Eily spread out a sheet on a bush to dry.

''Tis done!' Eily smiled and dried her hands on her apron, then stopped to rest for a few minutes. 'Isn't it a grand day, pet!'

The soft wind that would dry the clothes caught at the strands of Mary-Brigid's fair hair, tossing it in every direction. 'Twas a torment how her hair always ended up in tangles and knots, while her mother's fine hair was so easily patted into place. She watched as her mother's gaze took in the land and fields all around them.

'See those walls, Mary-Brigid? Your daddy's daddy, Grandaddy Joshua, and *his* daddy built those stone walls. They had to dig the rocks and stones from under the earth and lift them, and they got more rocks from the riverbank, then they laid them one by one on top of each other. It took them a long, long time.'

Mary-Brigid ran her eyes along the low, grey stone walls, each stone balanced perfectly with another, that formed the boundary of their small farm, with its potato field, the rough hilly pasture, and the stony patch where her mother's vegetables and a square of wheat fought to grow. Her Daddy and Mammy worked so hard, clearing the soil, planting it and weeding it. Mostly Daddy had to work for the landlord, of course, tending to their own land only when he could get a minute free.

In the distance, Muck, the pig they were fattening for winter, squealed hungrily from the ramshackle pigpen.

'We'd better get him some scraps and peelings soon,' Eily said, 'or he'll scream the place down.'

They picked up the washbasket, took a handle each, and strolled back towards the neat little homestead, with its pile of dry turf, the curl of smoke from the chimney, and the bright, shining window pane winking and catching the sunlight.

'Shoo! Shoo!' Mary-Brigid told the hens who ran and pecked in front of her. Maisie, her favourite red hen, tried, as usual, to follow her into the shade of the kitchen. That old hen was far too cute for her own good, Auntie Nano often said. Nano lay dozing now, her rocking chair still, in front of the fire.

'Ssh, Mammy!' warned Mary-Brigid, 'she's asleep!'

'Ssh!' echoed her little brother Jodie, imitating her. He looked up from where he had been playing quietly in the corner of the room.

Their great grand-aunt looked so peaceful there, snoring ever so slightly.

'There might be some honey for you two later,' whispered Eily. 'Daddy is going to check the beehive for the both of ye.' The children adored honey – a little bit spread on the fresh bread Eily baked, or spooned into their bowls of porridge, was the best treat possible. They licked their lips at the very thought of it.

Eily was always thinking of little things to please the children and make them happy. When she was a girl times had been very hard, and Auntie Nano said that she had never forgotten it.

'Now, pet, will you do me a favour and take Jodie out to play in the fresh air!'

Jodie ran up to Mary-Brigid, his sturdy two-year-old hands grabbing at her skirt as he followed her outside.

'Stay near the house, Mary-Brigid!' warned Eily. 'None of your gallivanting or exploring, now.'

Mary-Brigid sighed. She'd had a mind to go down to the stream to look for pinkeens.

'Come on, Jodie!' she said. 'We'll just have to find something else to do!'

Jodie nodded his curly brown head. As little brothers went, Mary-Brigid guessed that Jodie wasn't the worst. He knew how to play chasing, though he was so slow at running, and he was good at playing baby princes that Mary-Brigid had to rescue from all sorts of monsters and evil lords.

Maisie clucked about and followed them, pecking busily as she went.

'Hen! Hen!' announced Jodie, pointing a grubby finger at the bird.

'That's Maisie, Jodie. Say MAAII-SSEE!'

'HEN!' repeated her brother solemnly.

'But Maisie is much more than just an ordinary old hen,' said Mary-Brigid dramatically, hunkering down on the grass, as the dusty hen scratched at the ground. 'Maisie is a *magic* hen!' Mary-Brigid's eyes twinkled.

Jodie stood in front of his sister, his fingers opening and closing in a futile attempt to clutch at the darting bundle of rich brown-red feathers that jumped and fluttered to escape him.

'She lays golden eggs,' Mary-Brigid continued, dropping her voice, 'and she can see the *sidhe*!' But Jodie ignored her. He didn't know anything about the fairies; he was much more interested in catching the creature.

Maisie pecked away, keeping just out of range of the two of them.

'Jodie, if we're good and quiet,' Mary Brigid went on, 'Maisie might lead us to one of her eggs, her special golden eggs.'

A shadow of confusion passed across Jodie's small face. He liked eggs, though what eggs had to do with this clucking creature, he wasn't sure. But he followed his big sister, as she raced after Maisie, who was now squawking wildly and running madly in all directions.

*   *   *

'You'd think the child had been caught in a thorn bush, John! Just look at the state of him!' Eily was furious. 'Look at the clothes I washed yesterday!'

Mary-Brigid kept her eyes on the dripping square of potato cake on her plate. What was all the fuss about? Jodie had only a few scratches and scrapes. She could see that her father was trying not to smile.

'Do you know anything about this, Mary-Brigid?' John asked solemnly.

Mary-Brigid shrugged her shoulders and licked the smear of butter from her lips.

'I thought I saw the two of you chasing that yoke of a hen this afternoon,' he added.

'MAASSEE!' pronounced Jodie, trying at the same time to flap his arms like the hen. Everyone burst out laughing.

'You two rogues!' teased their father, tousling Mary-Brigid's wild mop of hair and sticking the tip of his little finger into one of the dimples on her cheek. 'My laughing girl!'

'Thank God for the food on the table,' Nano broke in, 'and for the family and children to share it with.'

'Amen,' answered Eily softly.

*   *   *

Mary-Brigid stared into the flickering flames of the turf-and-wood fire. Sitting hunched on a cushion in her nightclothes, she pushed her bare toes and feet close to the heat, watching the shadows from the flames dance around the room. The regular creak of Nano's heavy rocking chair was the only sound in the silence of the small cottage.

Eily was busy putting Jodie to bed, and John had gone out to check the animals.

Mary-Brigid blew softly on the low fire.

'What are you doing, child?' asked Nano.

'I'm just giving a bit of life to the fire.'

'You know you must be careful of the fire, dote. Come and sit by me, and let a bit of the heat out to my old bones.'

Mary-Brigid crouched beside Nano. Her great grand-aunt was the oldest and nicest person she knew.

'Nano,' said Mary-Brigid, tossing the tumble of blond hair from her face and resting her cheek on the old woman's lap, 'Nano, will you tell me a story?'

The old lady sighed, not an exasperated sigh, but the sigh of one used to such a request from a favourite child.

'Well, what kind of story would you be wanting, then?' asked Nano, her soft blue eyes shining and the lines around them creasing. 'Is it ghosts or goblins you want?'

Mary-Brigid considered. 'No! Not that kind of story tonight, Nano. The story of long ago.'

'Ah!' said Nano, 'of high kings and warriors and great deeds!'

'No!' frowned Mary-Brigid. 'The story of Mammy and Michael and Peggy.'

'Ah!' sighed Nano, shifting herself in the chair, '*that* story.' The child was always pestering her for that story.

''Tis a story of courage,' began Nano softly. Mary-Brigid nodded, her dark eyes shining. 'A story of a sister and a brother and a wee slip of a girl about your own age. The times were hard then, so hard. You see, the potato crop had failed. The people dug their crop only to discover that everything had turned to slime. Now everyone knew that as sure as night follows day the hunger would come. From cabin to cabin, cottage to cottage, across the fields and farms of Ireland, they knew. And they waited.'

Eily slipped back into the room. Leaning against the door she listened, as Nano's hushed voice went on, 'Your Mammy and Uncle Michael and Auntie Peggy didn't want to go to the workhouse with the rest, so Eily decided that they would run away, across the countryside, and try to find Lena and myself.'

Eily closed her eyes as she heard again the story of her youth ...

CHAPTER 2

Castletaggart Stables

MICHAEL O'DRISCOLL TURNED IN HIS SLEEP, trying to get comfortable on the hard, wooden pallet bed.

'Michael! Wake up! Do ye hear me! Will ya get up!'

Michael groaned, pulling the blanket up around his shoulders.

'Get up, Michael, get up quick! It's Ragusa, she's having her foal. Toss said I was to come and get you.'

Michael rubbed the sleep from his eyes and began to pull himself out of bed. He fumbled around, searching for his boots and his jacket in the near-pitch dark of the stable lads' quarters over the coach-house. Why did mares always give birth in the dead of night!

Young Brendan Foley, at thirteen the youngest and greenest of the stable lads, stood impatiently in front of Michael, holding the paraffin lamp, its aura of yellow light swinging backwards and forwards, catching a startled mouse as it scampered away.

'She's bad, Michael, Toss is ...'

'Hold the lamp still!' ordered Michael, searching for his second boot.

'He's real worried about her!'

'It's too soon and she's getting too old,' muttered Michael tersely. Anger bubbled inside him. Ragusa was one of the finest mares in the stable. She deserved better than this. They crept in silence along the narrow upstairs room, trying not to disturb the other lads. Then they climbed down the steep wooden stairs that led out into the yard. The horses were quiet, but one or two whinnied as they passed. It was still deep night outside, with a good while to go till dawn. A heavy swag of dark cloud masked the moon.

As he pushed in the stable door, Michael could hear Toss's voice murmuring softly to the mare. The pregnant mare lay on the straw and, by the look of her, she was already exhausted.

Michael leant down and patted her neck. 'Good girl! 'Tis all right, girl, you'll be fine.'

From her eyes he could tell she was scared. The mare herself could sense that all was not well. Michael grabbed some straw and wiped her down a bit.

'She hasn't much push left in her, Michael,' said Toss anxiously. 'She's not trying. The foal needs more help.'

Michael nodded.

'Brendan, get us some water!' ordered Toss.

The young lad was back in a minute or two with a heavy tin bucket full of water.

Toss was walking around the mare, looking at her closely, and Michael could sense his concern. Toss was the best horseman that Michael had ever met. Anything Michael knew about horses so far he had learnt from the sixty-year-old man.

Toss had spent all his life with horses. He had worked all over – in Cork, in Wicklow, in England. It didn't matter where, once there were good horses there and a good owner or manager. For the past fifteen years, Toss had worked at Castletaggart House. Michael felt sure that Toss had helped him get the position of stable lad, then assistant with the horses and occasional jockey.

After so many years working together, there was no need for words between them. They both knew the danger the ageing mare was in as she struggled to give life to yet another foal.

'I told him! You heard me, Michael! I told him it was too soon after the last foal. That she was getting on.' Michael could sense the deep anger in Toss's voice when he talked about the estate manager, George Darker. 'He should have listened to me.'

Ragusa whinnied. Her whole body was taut with pain. Michael washed his hands and arms in the cold water, and then knelt down to examine her gently. He could feel the foal – the strong curve of its spine, the long, thin bones of its legs and the slant of its head. The muzzle was down. The small foal badly needed help.

'Toss, if you and Brendan steady Ragusa, I'll try and pull the foal,' Michael said.

He caught the thin legs between the knees and fetlocks and eased the foal gently outwards. He listened carefully to Toss, who was guiding him in time with the mare's spasms. Michael held firmly onto the cannon bones. After a long time the brown legs were out.

The mare tried to roll, but Toss and young Brendan held her as Michael firmly drew the head and neck of the foal out. Seconds later, the skinny colt foal lay steaming hot and new and quivering on the straw.

Ragusa, lifeless now, raised her head and neck momentarily to look at her newest foal, her gentle brown eyes searching for him. Then she lay back, her whole body overcome with trauma. It took only a few seconds for the old mare to die, as Michael and Toss and Brendan watched helplessly. The foal lay on the straw, bewildered, sniffing at his mother's legs, waiting for her to clean and nuzzle him.

Toss stood up, his grey hair standing on end, his chin and cheeks covered in a grey stubble. 'Well, she's done for! One of the best mares that ever ran! As for the colt, it won't survive without her. It's too small, born too early. Ragusa and her foal – that's some night's work!'

Toss couldn't contain his grief any longer. His eyes filled with tears. 'Let me out of here!' he shouted angrily, stepping over the mare's body and across the straw. 'You two see to things,' he ordered gruffly as he strode into the yard, and went off in the direction of his small lodgings on the far side of the stable buildings.

Michael knew what would happen. Toss would get wildly drunk and not be seen for a day or two. He was blaming himself.

'What should we do?' Michael was brought back to the present dilemma by Brendan. The colt was trying to put one long, scrawny leg in front of another, making every effort to stand and get closer to his mother. 'Ah Michael! What are we supposed to do?' sniffed Brendan.

Michael considered. Ragusa was dead. He had to stifle his feelings of sadness and think of the foal, the orphan foal he'd helped to deliver. There was not much two young fellas like themselves could do, and yet the thought of watching the young foal lie there on the straw and weaken and die was too much to take. He couldn't stomach it. There must be something they could try.

'Brendan, have we any other mares in foal at the moment?'

The young lad pondered, mentally running through the different stables he mucked out each day.

'No!' he said regretfully. 'There are two, but they're only starting.'

The colt tried to stand on his wobbly legs, and managed to take a step or two. He nosed curiously at his mother, wondering why she was barely warm, wondering why the heavy rhythm of her regular, familiar heartbeat had suddenly stopped.

'What about weaning?' asked Michael in desperation. 'Any mares –'

Before he could finish, Brendan broke in, 'There's Glengarry! She finished up maybe ten days ago.'

'You stay here with the colt, don't let him get cold.' Michael picked up an enamel mug and rinsed it in the water bucket, then he stepped out of the stable into the cold early-morning air. Soon it would be dawn. He yawned, gulping in the fresh air to try and keep himself awake.

Glengarry shared her stable with another mare. She

was a solid chestnut with a white blaze on her face. She lifted her ears and looked at Michael intelligently, wondering why he was disturbing her sleep. Her stable companion whinnied in annoyance.

'Good girl! Good girl!' said Michael, kneeling down on Glengarry's bedding and trying to push her over sideways so he could see if she was still producing milk. She didn't seem to be. Then he felt her udder and pressed on one of her teats, watching as the moisture swelled it. She just might be able to feed the foal.

But how would he get her to accept Ragusa's foal? Michael wondered. Mares were only interested in their own foals. Her blanket lay on a hook behind the door. He'd try that and perhaps some of her bedding.

He looked at Glengarry. Surely she would be a good foster-mother? It was his only chance.

He tried to milk her, but there was very little milk and most of it seeped onto his hands. The rest made a tiny pool in the enamel mug. Grabbing the blanket and some bedding, he left, closing the door carefully behind him.

He could hear Brendan's voice as he approached Ragusa's door. The boy was singing to the colt. The young animal looked shaky and cold, and the young boy almost as bad. 'He's going downhill, Michael, I didn't know what to do.'

'It's all right, Brendan, I've an idea. But I need you to help me. Here, take this blanket. I want you to rub it all over the foal – try and get some of the oil from the blanket on to him.'

The foal lay still as the two of them rubbed his coat all over. Then Michael dipped his fingers in the mare's milk and spread it over the young animal's head and neck, wetting his nose area thoroughly. He wiped his hands along the dark mane and fine, brown-coloured coat of the bay colt, soaking the scared creature, who was now sniffing desperately at his fingers. Finally, they rubbed the scrawny hooves and legs in the bedding from Glengarry's stable.

'Ready!' said Michael.

Brendan nodded and the two of them half-carried and half-walked the brand new colt to meet his foster mother. The bewildered young foal shivered as they crossed the cobbled yard, the pale, dipping moon reflecting in his shiny eyes.

The mare whinnied, smelling the strange animal as soon as they entered her stable. Michael told Brendan to leave the foal down on the straw a few yards from the mare. Then they both stood back, over at the door, watching silently, keeping the lamp almost out of sight.

Nothing happened. The mare ignored the foal and the foal stayed weakly where he was.

'Should we lift him over to her?' urged Brendan.

'No! Wait! Give them more time!' whispered Michael.

They waited and waited.

After what seemed an age the mare got up and shook herself slowly, then she ambled over to look at the foal. Michael was worried in case Glengarry would nip at the orphan, but she simply ran her nose very lightly over the small form. Then, much to the boys' disappointment, she turned her back on the foal and stood chewing at some hay.

'Oh no!' groaned Brendan.

'Ssh!' said Michael. 'Wait!'

The foal lay still on the straw. He seemed ready to just roll over and go to sleep, when suddenly he tried to push himself up on one leg then another, until he was finally standing. He was badly balanced and he knew it. Very shakily, he brought himself alongside the mare. Glengarry put down her head and began to sniff him – his back, his shoulders, his breast, his legs, running her soft nose along his coat, taking in his scent. Then she nuzzled his head. The foal balanced anxiously against her chest and belly. She nipped at him slightly. Then, taking her time, she nuzzled his head again, recognising her own scent, her own milk, before lifting her head and letting him suckle. The foal seemed confused, but he was hungry and exhausted and weak.

There was very little milk, but the small colt had begun to feed.

Michael sighed with relief. Brendan punched his fist in the air and mouthed a silent Yes!

'That's the grandest thing I ever saw,' whispered Brendan, his voice filled with admiration.

Michael smiled. Brendan reminded him a lot of himself at that age. The lad liked animals and was kind to them.

'We're not out of the woods yet, Brendan. She might still reject him, you know, and we can only hope she has enough milk to feed him.'

'Oh!' Brendan's face fell.

'Come on, we'll try and get a bit of sleep before the early ride-out.'

The two stable lads quietly closed the door on the mare and the new foal and walked back towards the upstairs rooms where they slept. Morning light streaked across the sky and signalled the start of yet another busy day.

Ragusa's stable lay silent. Michael glanced over at it as he climbed the narrow, creaking stairs, and wondered how could life and death be so closely connected on that one night.

CHAPTER 3

Morning Boy

TOSS WAS IN TROUBLE with George Darker over the loss of the valuable mare. He railed against the unfairness of it all and shouted back at the estate manager, who had not listened to his original warnings about Ragusa.

Lord Buckland himself arrived down at the stables. He had liked Ragusa. 'A good horse!' he said sadly. 'Won a few good races in her day and we've bred many a fine filly from her.'

But this didn't stop them sending for the knackers' cart to come and take her away. Michael made sure that young Brendan was busy elsewhere; the lad was upset enough.

Miss Felicia, the youngest daughter of the house, appeared in the stables too. She'd heard there was a new foal. Strict instructions had been given that there was to be no mention of the demise of Ragusa. Nothing was to spoil the eleven-year-old's enjoyment at seeing the new horse.

'I thought the mare's stable was there!' Felicia said to Michael, pointing to Ragusa's empty stable. Michael didn't say a word.

The young girl clapped when she saw the bay colt and the chestnut mare standing close together.

'Oh, he's lovely! Just so perfect! But he's not one bit like his mother!' she declared

'Perhaps he's more like his father,' offered Michael, trying to make light of it.

He liked Miss Felicia. She spent half of her time in the stables and was a proper little tomboy. Her older sister, Rose, was about Michael's own age and a beauty, but she rarely set foot in the stableyard unless it was to request a carriage. She had no interest whatsoever in horses, or in the stable lads and grooms and jockeys who worked for her father.

'Michael! Didn't you hear me? Which do you think is the finest horse in my father's stables?' enquired Felicia, letting the new foal nuzzle at her fingers.

'Well, that I'm not sure of, Miss, it would depend on what you'd be wanting the horse for. Samson and Jolly are two of the best farmhorses you'd ever get, and your father's pair of greys are considered the finest carriage horses in the county. Your father loves Old Tom when he wants to go out on a day's hunting – he says rain or wind or sleet, Old Tom never lets him down. And you ... well, do you remember that you had a great shine for Markey?'

'Markey isn't a horse,' the girl spluttered. 'Markey's a donkey.'

'Well, that didn't seem to matter when you were small and you'd be sneaking him carrots and apples.'

Felicia giggled. 'Which do you think?' she insisted, tossing her auburn curls off her face.

'Some of them are fast. Jerpoint's very fast. Nero's won four races already and Toss feels that Juno might have a good chance this season.'

'And?'

'Well, I like this youngster,' he said, nodding towards the colt.

Felicia ran her white palm along the foal's coat. 'He's a bit small and a bit wobbly,' she stated, 'but I like him too. What's he called?'

Michael shrugged. 'He was only born early this morning, Miss. Toss hasn't had time to discuss it with your father yet.'

'This morning!'

Michael nodded, trying to block out memories of Ragusa.

'Then ... I think we should call him Morning – Morning Boy. I'll tell Father.'

Michael smiled. Whatever that young lady suggested, her father usually agreed to. Having no sons, Henry Buckland was besotted by his two daughters, especially Felicia, who followed him around like an over-eager puppy.

'Felicia! You are to come into the house immediately!' They both turned at the same time to see Rose standing at the gate to the cobbled yard. 'Mary is running you a bath and you are to get changed. Mother is very vexed with you.'

'I'll be along in a minute,' Felicia muttered in annoyance, kissing the middle of Morning Boy's nose.

'Now!' insisted her older sister, reluctant to walk across the cobbles in case she stood in some horse dung.

Felicia turned on her toes. 'Rose Geranium Cowslip Buckland, I'll be with you *right now!*' she shouted.

Michael tried to hide his smile. Miss Felicia reminded him so much of his younger sister, Peggy. Full of spirit. Poor Rose had turned the colour of a turkey-cock and was walking as fast as she could, skirt flying, back up the avenue. At the top of the rhododendron-lined avenue stood the big house.

Michael remembered when, as a young lad, he had

first come to work in the stables of Castletaggart House. He had found it so hard to believe that anyone could live in such a grand place, with its hundreds of sparkling window-panes and stonework ledges and wide granite steps. In the six years since he'd come to work at the big house Michael had learnt so much – not only about horses, but about the big house and its ways.

At first Toss had only let him clean out the stables, just mucking out, the very worst job in the place. Michael begged for the chance to ride the horses and was overwhelmed with disappointment at each refusal. Still, Toss had no complaints about his work.

'I'm watching you!' was all Toss would say.

Obviously, Michael had to show his ability before he would be trusted with any of the Buckland horses. In time, Toss gave him his chance.

There was no doubt that Castletaggart House was the finest house ever and Lord Henry Buckland a very wealthy man. Every fish that swam in the river and lake, every cow that grazed on the vast green fields, every pheasant and woodcock that inhabited the under-growth, every apple or cabbage that grew from the rich brown soil was part of the vast Buckland estate. There were about forty tenants' cottages on the estate for the workers and their families. The tenant farmers worked the estate lands and in return were given a patch of ground where they could only grow barely enough to feed their own families.

Michael would watch these men – young, middle-aged and old – come cap-in-hand to the estate manager's office, queuing outside to pay their rent and hand over their dues. They reminded him of his father long ago, that same wooden look in their faces, their eyes set, their hearts hardened. They probably had ignored the pleas of wives and children to hold a few shillings back in case the winter was hard, or the sickness came – or worse, God forbid, that the potatoes would fail again. No, these men would pay their way and hand over the money they earned, the crops they grew, the animals they raised. They had no choice.

George Darker, the estate manager, would write down the figures in big brown ledgers. He was barely civil to them, stubbing the page with a dirty finger to show where they were to sign their name or make their mark.

Sometimes Lord Henry, if he was in the mood, would join them, puffing his pipe, making polite conversation with the men.

Michael could sense a growing feeling of unease amongst these tenant farmers. He listened as they talked between themselves, behind cabin doors and in crowded public houses. Michael wondered what would come of all this talk. These men wanted change ...

'Michael! Are you listening to me?'

Michael looked down.

Felicia was gazing up at him, impatient. 'I'll be back down to see Morning Boy tomorrow afternoon, after my lessons.'

'That's fine, Miss.'

She raced across the yard, swinging on the open gate, and humming to herself as she tried to catch up with her sister and make amends.

CHAPTER 4

The Visit

MARY-BRIGID LOVED TO GO visiting even if it did mean having to get her hair brushed and pulled and braided back into two tight plaits. She swung her head from side to side, feeling the comforting wallop of hair against her cheek as she followed her mother along the bumpy laneway towards the Hennessys' cottage. Eily walked briskly, carrying Jodie on her hip. The hedgerows were covered in heavy red droopy fuchsia bushes, and beneath them clumps of spiky orange flowers sprang out everywhere. It was a grand day for a walk and their friends' cottage was only about another half-mile away. Mary-Brigid was looking forward to seeing the Hennessy boys again – it was a while since school had closed for the holidays and she missed her friends.

The Hennessys' cottage was a bit bigger than their own, but as they came near it Mary-Brigid couldn't help but notice that some of the thatch needed patching and the windows needed mending. She waited patiently as her mother called at the open door. 'Hello, Frances! God bless all here.' They went into the turf-smelling, untidy kitchen.

'Eily! I'm right glad to see you and the children,' said Frances Hennessy. 'And how's Mary-Brigid, the best girl in these parts?'

'Fine, thank you, Mrs Hennessy!' Mary-Brigid replied shyly.

'Sit ye down! Sit ye down!' Frances was busy feeding Colm, her youngest boy, who, with his scattering of pale ginger curls and freckled nose, was the very image of his mother. 'I'll wet the tea in a few minutes.'

Jodie disappeared off straight away to play with little Eoin, who was much the same age as himself. But Mary-Brigid's friends, the twins, were nowhere to be seen, so she sat quiet and embarrassed as her mother and Frances chatted.

'The twins will be along in a minute, pet,' said Frances, 'and they have something special to show you.' She laughed, flinging back her plump neck and ignoring the dirty floor and mess of unwashed clothes in a heap in the corner. She was delighted with her visitors.

'The fire's a bit low, Mary-Brigid, will you be a good child and run out and fetch in a bit of turf for us?'

At the side of the house, Mary-Brigid looked at the sorry pile of dried-out old turf which lay on the ground. Her own daddy worked up on the bog as often as he could and already had a pile of turf almost the height of the chimney stacked against their house for the winter. The Hennessys would have to get a lot more turf, as they certainly hadn't enough here to get them through the year. She selected four pieces that weren't too crumbly and carried them inside, where her mother and Frances were deep in conversation.

'There isn't a spare penny, Eily. Paddy won't even organise himself to cut enough turf to keep us going when the bad weather comes.' Frances sounded really upset now.

'Maybe John could bring some over for you,' offered Eily. 'We have plenty.'

'That's kind of you. Poor Paddy isn't himself at the moment.' Frances was almost in tears. 'The new landlord came over here with William Hussey, his agent, and the two of them gave Paddy a right going over about yields and about that thistle field out back.

'Everyone hereabouts knows that that field has grown nothing but thistles for years,' she went on. 'The agent said that Paddy's not working the land properly,

not growing enough crops, not paying enough rent ...
I tell you, Eily, Paddy's right upset about it, angry like;
there's no telling what fool idea he'll get into his head.'

Mary-Brigid tried to concentrate and understand
what they were talking about. She could tell by her
mother's face and voice that it was something bad.

'This new landlord, Frances, what's he like?' Eily
asked.

'Dennis Ormonde? A quare fellow!' said Frances. 'He
wants us to work like slaves so that we can pay him a
higher rent.'

'A higher rent!' gasped Eily.

'Aye! Paddy's right worried that Hussey is going to
try and make us surrender our holding and evict us!'

'He couldn't do that! He wouldn't!' cried Eily.

'Mark my words, Eily, there's no telling what that
man will do to the tenants!' Frances said angrily,
shaking her head of wavy curls.

A clatter of noise disrupted the conversation as the
twins, Pascal and Patsy, appeared at last. They both
looked grimy and dishevelled, but that didn't matter a
bit to Mary-Brigid. She jumped up to join them and get
away from the serious conversation of the mothers.

'Mam, can we bring Mary-Brigid to see Mo?' they
asked.

'Aye!' nodded their mother, who had brightened at

the sight of the two nine-year-old rascals. 'I'm trusting you boys to take good care of her, and keep her out of trouble.' A puzzled look filled their identical features, as if they would never dream of getting into trouble!

'Arragh! Run off the three of ye,' said Frances with a laugh, 'and give Eily and meself a bit of peace!'

*   *   *

Mary-Brigid was out of breath after an hour or more of haring around with the twins as they showed her everything – the muddy pool near the ditch where some frogs lived, the huge oak tree that Patsy said he'd climbed to see a crows' nest, and the well which was so deep that if you dropped a stone in, you couldn't hear it land. But the twins kept the very best thing to last. Mo, the farm cat, had had kittens and they took Mary-Brigid down to the old out-house to see them.

The very minute she set eyes on the four small bundles of fur, lying close to their large marmalade-coloured mother, Mary-Brigid fell in love with them.

'Would you like to hold one of them?' asked Patsy.

Mary-Brigid nodded. One bold little fellow got up from the old sacking bed and came over to sniff at her fingers and let itself be stroked. She could feel the orange kitten's tiny claws stick to the wool of her cardigan as she hugged it close.

'You're my favourite!' whispered Mary-Brigid in its ear, as the kitten stretched its paw to claw at her plait of hair. She wanted to hold this little kitten and never let it go.

It was nearly tea-time when they ran back to the cottage.

'We're starving, Mammy!' shouted the boys.

'Will ye stay, Eily, and have a bite with us?' offered Frances.

'Thank you kindly, Frances, but I've left Nano keeping an eye on a pot of rabbit stew,' said Eily.

Mary-Brigid could sense her mother's tiredness and anxiety.

'Try not to worry, Frances,' Eily continued, 'the Tenants' Rights League would never let William Hussey get his way. Look, I'll send John over in the morning with the cart of turf, and maybe he can talk to Paddy.'

The two young women hugged each other.

'You're a good friend, Eily,' murmured Frances, tears welling in her eyes, 'I'll never forget you for this!' She turned to the twins. 'Patsy, did ye get what I told you?'

The twins disappeared but returned within seconds, carrying the orange kitten which they tumbled into Mary-Brigid's delighted arms.

'What do you say, Mary-Brigid?' prompted Eily.

'Thank you! Oh, thank you so much, Mrs Hennessy.

I promise to take good care of him.'

The Hennessys stood at their door until Eily, Mary-Brigid and Jodie were out of sight. Eily was silent and distracted, Jodie drowsy and almost asleep on her shoulder, as they traipsed along the path for home. Mary-Brigid did her best to block out the words and worries she'd overheard with the comforting heat of the small kitten cradled inside her cardigan.

'Just wait till Maisie sees him!' she announced.

CHAPTER 5

Greenbay, Boston

PEGGY O'DRISCOLL WAS JADED, just jaded. She had washed and scrubbed and polished every floor and door and piece of furniture in Rushton House, in Greenbay, Boston. She had worked from sun-up to sun-down for the past week. Poor Mrs O'Connor, the cook, lay flopped down in her big kitchen chair, out cold with exhaustion. Normally, Peggy would have giggled at her loud snores, but today she knew that Cook, like the rest of them, was worn out with the preparations for Miss Roxanne's wedding.

Kitty, the other maid, was all uppity, as she was helping Roxanne to prepare her trousseau and pack her things and organise her wedding gifts.

Peggy dawdled in the kitchen, helping herself to a

glass of cold water and an oatmeal biscuit.

'Mrs O'Connor! Mrs O'Connor!' She shook the woman's arm gently. 'Maybe it's time for bed!'

The old cook yawned. 'Did I fall asleep again, Peggy?'

'Aye.'

'You know, Peggy, I'm done in. I'm not getting any younger. Thanks be to God that the Rowans have only one daughter to get wed! I wouldn't be able for a family of them!'

Peggy grimaced. A family of Roxannes! It didn't bear thinking about. Roxanne was one of the vainest and most annoying and most aggravating creatures ever; Mrs O'Connor said it was a miracle that she was getting married. What young man would put up with her tantrums and bossiness and constant preening and admiring herself?

Still, Roxanne had found him. His name was Fletcher P. Parker. Peggy had seen him a few times.

He was about eight years older than Roxanne and of about average height. He had curly fair hair and his skin was pale and slightly blotchy. He was an attorney-at-law and he came from Baltimore. He had concluded some business with Mr Rowan and had been invited to the house for dinner. Miss Roxanne sat beside him. He made pleasant conversation with her and as the meal progressed Peggy watched as the young mistress flirted outrageously with him.

'The fish took the bait,' was all Mrs O'Connor would say.

Mr and Mrs Rowan seemed to approve as Fletcher Parker escorted Roxanne to a round of balls and operas and dinner parties and picnics. This had culminated in their betrothal and now their marriage.

'Help me up from the chair, lassie! My hip is playing up on me again!'

Peggy helped Mrs O'Connor to her feet. Up close she could see the pattern of laughter-lines and wrinkles that covered the cook's plump, pink-toned face.

'Mrs O'Connor, I'll bring you a cup of tea in the morning before you get up. 'Twill be a long day tomorrow.'

'Thank you, Peggy child! That would be grand. You know, you're the kindest lassie I know.'

Peggy smiled to herself as they both left the darkened kitchen, the pantry and store cupboards full to bursting with all the fine food for tomorrow's wedding. She sighed as she climbed the narrow, wooden stairs to her attic bedroom. She hoped Kitty would be asleep already. She was too tired for chit-chat, especially about the wedding.

But Kitty was sitting on the bed, busy tying up her

normally straight fine hair with rags.

'Peggy! I need you to do some of the pieces at the back,' said Kitty brightly.

'It's too late!' yawned Peggy. 'Why're you doing your hair at this hour anyway?'

'I want to have a few curls tomorrow so it'll look softer,' said the other girl wistfully.

''Tisn't you that's getting married!' snapped Peggy.

'But I'm assisting her and that's special. I'm her right-hand woman,' Kitty said importantly

Peggy tried to stifle a laugh. 'Here, pass me a bit of that cloth, you silly old thing,' she said, and she grabbed a piece of her friend's mouse-brown hair and wrapped it around her finger before tying it with a tight bow.

'Peggy! I've something to tell you.'

'Hmm!' answered Peggy, picking out another piece of hair.

'Promise you won't get cross!'

'I promise.'

'Roxanne has asked me to go and work for herself and Mister Fletcher Parker in the new house in Baltimore.'

Peggy dropped the piece of hair. 'I hope you told her no, Kitty!'

A heavy silence hung between them.

'Well, that's just it, Peggy. I told her yes, that I'd like to go.'

'Why, you miserable little ... Are you crazy! Work for that shrew? She'll beat you black and blue and scream at you and make your life a misery.'

'But I'll be her personal maid, with higher wages, and sort of chief housekeeper too. They'll take on a cook and a skivvy. She said I can advise her on household management and the like.'

Peggy swallowed a bitter lump of jealousy. It was ridiculous – Kitty *advise* anyone! It was just too stupid.

'What about the household accounts and bills?' questioned Peggy.

'Well, Miss Roxanne intends to keep the books herself, but I should be able to manage the day-to-day stuff,' Kitty said. 'Thanks to you teaching me to read and write,' she added.

Tears came into Peggy's eyes. Kitty was going away and leaving her! 'Kitty! Won't you miss the house and Greenbay?' Peggy asked. But what she really wanted to say was, Won't you miss me?

'But I'll come here. Miss Roxanne will often come to visit her parents and naturally I'll travel with her.' Kitty looked shyly at her friend. 'And I'll still get to see you, Peggy. You don't think I'd forget about my best and dearest friend.'

Peggy swallowed hard. She looked around the small bedroom with its two brass beds and cold linoleum

floor. The washstand with its jug and bowl. The
window with the stiff catch, their eye on the world. The
glass pitcher with its now dried-out flowers. The two
samplers they had spent weeks working on, hanging
on the wall above their beds: BE GOOD SWEET MAID and
FRIENDSHIP IS A GIFT, worked in multicoloured embroi-
dery threads. Peggy couldn't imagine this room without
Kitty.

When Peggy had first arrived, homesick and miserable, missing her home in Ireland, it was Kitty who had
made her smile, and helped her settle into this new life.

'Oh God, Kitty, I'll miss you so much,' sobbed Peggy.
The two girls hugged each other. 'It'll be so lonesome
here without you.'

CHAPTER 6

The Wedding

SUNSHINE STREAMED ACROSS the whole of Greenbay and seemed to dance and jiggle through every window of Rushton House. The big house basked in the warmth of a special family day. The garden was heavy with blooms, and pink roses clung to the trellising and the bower, and trailed along near the front porch and across the terrace. Swags of cream magnolia blossoms decorated the huge trees in front of the house. The mistress had had a team of gardeners tending the lawns and filling the flower-beds for months, so now there wasn't a weed to be seen, only a blaze of stunning colour.

There's nothing like a summer wedding, thought Peggy wistfully, as she gazed across the beautiful gardens.

Kitty and herself had been up at the crack of dawn. Kitty was so excited you'd think she was to be bridesmaid or something, thought Peggy. They grabbed an early breakfast for themselves in the kitchen. The family had theirs on trays in their rooms, as the dining table and breakfast table were already laid for the wedding banquet.

Peggy couldn't stop herself yawning. She had hardly slept a wink, thinking of Kitty leaving.

The minute Mrs O'Connor stepped into the kitchen it was as if the whole household staff were sucked into a whirlwind.

Young Simon was sent up and down the stairs with cups of lemon tea for the ladies. He provided the kitchen staff with a running account of the goings-on upstairs: 'Momma has the vapours'; 'Roxanne says she thinks her feet have swollen and her shoes are too small'; 'Pappa is unable to find his new collar buttons!'

Mrs Whitman, the housekeeper, supervised the delivery of fresh flowers, cooled white wine, and last-minute wedding gifts and tokens, as well as showing the Rowan cousins, who had arrived to stay, to their rooms.

Luckily, Peggy caught Bonaparte, the scamp of a dog, hiding under the heavy linen tablecloth chewing a bit of old bone! Wouldn't that be a fine to-do for one of the guests, to put their hand down to pick up a napkin and discover a mouldy old dog's bone!

'Go outside, you bad dog!' shouted Peggy, and she watched as he scampered across the dining room and out through the french doors.

By mid-day steam ran down the kitchen walls and dripped onto the floor. Peggy had a go at it every now and then with the mop, but it was a waste of effort. All the doors were open in the hope of catching some little bit of cooling breeze.

No expense had been spared and there were joints of beef roasting, chicken coated in white, creamy sauce and lobster dripping in butter. There were baby new potatoes, corn and greens and all sorts of vegetables. No guest would leave the wedding table hungry – Mrs O'Connor had made sure of that. She surveyed the laden side-tables, where tarts and frosted cakes and heavy fruitcakes, sodden with brandy, fought for attention. Well satisfied, the cook beckoned to Peggy.

'I'm going up to change, Peggy, you keep an eye on things here.' Mrs O'Connor's blouse clung damply to her plump folds of skin and her face was hot and flushed with all the cooking. Peggy took the opportunity to flop down on a stool near the back door.

After a little while Mrs O'Connor returned, looking refreshed and wearing a crisp white cotton blouse.

'That's a bit better, Peggy, I feel like a new woman now. Come on, Miss Roxanne is dressed and ready.'

The cook and Peggy stepped out into the crowded hallway just as the bride came down the winding, polished stairs.

Peggy had to admit that Roxanne Rowan looked for all the world like an angel on this her wedding day. Her blond hair hung in soft waves around her face, the back part coiled and looped around a spray of rose-buds. Her dress was pure, soft, cream silk with tiny pearl buttons up the front and from cuff to elbow. The material clung to Roxanne's slim figure and swept back in folds at her feet. Her skin shone and her eyes were full of happiness.

An 'Aah!' of pleasure filled the air as the assembled household staff took in her beauty.

'Good luck, Miss Roxanne!' beamed Mrs O'Connor, hugging her.

'Every happiness to you and Mister Fletcher Parker,' said Miss Whitman, her thin face eager as she shook the bride's hand.

Peggy stood transfixed. It was her turn. Normally she would just mumble and say as little as possible to the girl who had once made her life so miserable – the girl who had teased and jeered her and even accused her of stealing. A slight blush of colour came into the other girl's cheeks. Peggy lifted her eyes to meet the pale blue of Roxanne's. There she saw happiness and hope and nervousness and sadness all jumbled together. They were no longer enemies.

'I wish you happiness and many, many good things in the future, Miss Roxanne, I really do!' said Peggy warmly.

Roxanne smiled. 'Thank you, Peggy, I appreciate it,' she said, shaking Peggy's hand before moving on to the next person.

Peggy blinked, surprised at herself. She really had meant it. She wished only happiness for this girl who was leaving her mother and father and going off to make a new life for herself with Mr Fletcher Parker. Kitty, who was standing on the stairs, caught Peggy's eye and winked.

Mr Fletcher Parker and his family and the other guests were already outdoors in the beautiful summer gardens of Rushton, for that was where the marriage ceremony would take place. A shady spot had been chosen and the Reverend Samuel Brooke stood waiting there.

A hush fell over the garden as Roxanne, holding her father's arm, walked out to join her future husband. Back in the kitchen Peggy and Kitty and Mrs O'Connor stood at the open door listening to the simple words

of the bible drifting across the hedge as Roxanne
Rowan was wed. Then Peggy and Kitty moved outside,
offering the guests a glass of cooling summer punch
before the meal was served.

Peggy felt such a stab of loneliness as she watched
cousins and aunts, and uncles and grandchildren, all
hug and greet each other. She thought of Eily and
Michael, and Aunt Nano and all of them – her own
family so far away from her.

Mr Fletcher Parker stood beside the bride. For once
he looked actually handsome, as they both welcomed
and conversed with their guests. Laughter filled the
house, both inside and out, as family and friends joined
in celebrating Roxanne's wedding day.

The sun was sinking and lamps lit up the dark
outside when the first guests began to slip away.
Peggy's back and shoulders ached after the long day
and she longed to sit down and rest. Mrs O'Connor
flopped in the kitchen chair, and thanked God that
everything had gone so well. Many compliments had
been paid to the cook, and her choice of menu had
been considered very wise.

Peggy and Kitty and Miss Whitman stared in disbelief
at the huge pile of dirty plates and glasses and servers
still to be washed. Wearily they re-filled the kitchen
sink with water and Peggy washed and scrubbed for

what seemed like hours, with Kitty drying and Miss Whitman putting the dishes away.

Peggy had no idea what hour it was when they eventually climbed the stairs to the attic. Kitty, still wearing her uniform, fell onto her bed, pulled up the light sheet and was asleep in a second, her unsteady snores annoying Peggy. Peggy was about to jump up and shake her friend when she realised that soon Kitty would be gone and there'd come a time when she would miss even the snores of her fellow-maid.

CHAPTER 7

The Widow O'Brien

'MAMMY! COME QUICKLY!' shouted Mary-Brigid. 'All the neighbours are walking up the boreen!' She ran as fast as she could up the stony path to the house, dying to tell the news.

Her mother put down the greasy pot she was scrubbing, and, dipping her hands in some clean water, came to the door to see what was happening. She could just make out the backs of a group of people disappearing around the gentle curve of the boreen.

'What did they say, pet?' she asked, anxious.

'They said 'tis a viction, Mammy. What does that mean?' asked Mary-Brigid, her dark eyes puzzled.

Her mother put her hand to her face, covering her mouth. Surely the child must have got it wrong.

'What is it, Eily? What's the child on about?' enquired Nano, rising awkwardly from the kitchen table where she was kneading dough.

'There's something going on a bit up the road, Nano. I think I'll go and see,' said Eily, pulling off her damp apron, and adjusting the comb in her coiled-up hair.

'Wait a minute, Eily, and I'll be along with you,' said Nano. 'We'll take the children too. Mary-Brigid, pass me my shawl from behind the door!'

Mary-Brigid sensed the urgency and foreboding that passed between her mother and Nano as they closed the cottage door behind them and followed in the direction of the others.

'What is it, Mammy, what's a viction?'

'Just you keep quiet for a few minutes, Mary-Brigid, till we see what all the fuss is about!' snapped her mother.

Mary-Brigid was right vexed with her and fell into step alongside Nano. Her old auntie was slow enough at walking these days but she still loved a bit of fresh air.

'This will put roses in our cheeks, Mary-Brigid!' murmured Nano, her pure white hair and sturdy, black-clad figure bending down towards the child.

Mary-Brigid couldn't help smiling and putting her fingers to her cheeks. 'Are they rosy yet?' she joked.

Both Eily and Nano burst out laughing.

But all the merriment disappeared the minute they turned the corner. Over the thick green hedgerow they spotted the small crowd gathering outside the Widow O'Brien's simple, one-roomed cottage. There was no denying the cottage was neglected, with weeds fighting to grow up over it, dirt and moss clinging to it, and the rotting thatch almost bare in places.

In front of the cottage were three men on horseback. Two were constables, the third was the bailiff.

Mary-Brigid grabbed hold of her mother's hand as fear washed over her. 'What are they going to do?'

'We'll know soon enough, pet,' Eily whispered, putting her arm protectively around her daughter.

'Failure to pay rent,' shouted the bailiff, a big lump of a man with a bald head. 'Failure to follow acquittal notice! Failure to maintain dwelling! Failure to develop and maintain allotted land-holding!'

'God almighty!' muttered Eily. 'A poor soul like Agnes O'Brien, a widow woman all on her own being evicted! 'Tis a disgrace!'

The crowd murmured, drawing in close around the cottage, flattening the thigh-high weeds.

'Leave her alone! She's only a poor old woman!' shouted one of the men.

'Let her be!' added more voices angrily.

'We're only doing our duty,' replied the younger of the constables. 'The old lady has known for quite some time that she would have to give up this dwelling.' He blushed, embarrassed.

Nano pulled at Eily's arm, nodding in the direction of the small, grubby window. They could just make out the white, scared face of Agnes O'Brien peeping out.

The bailiff banged on the door again.

'Let her be!' shouted Tim Hayes. 'What use is a cabin like that to anyone? Let her stay there, no one else would be interested in it.'

'I'll 'mind you to look after your own business, Mr Hayes,' sneered the bailiff. 'Mister Hussey plans to plough up this whole piece of land, not that that is any of your concern.'

Mary-Brigid stood silent, wishing that her daddy or more of the men were here to help. Unfortunately, he had gone to the bog to turn and dry out more turf for the winter.

'It's the only home poor Agnes has ever known!' said Nano loudly. 'She'll be afraid leaving it. Her two sons were born under that roof. She nursed her family when they all got fever in that one room, managing to feed them on scraps and meal and berries and roots.'

There was a hush now as the muttering stopped and the whole crowd paid attention to Nano. 'It was through that little bit of a door that the boys left to go to America and two years later that her husband, God be good to him, was brought out when he died. Agnes thought she'd follow on after him in her turn. She never imagined the like of this happening.' Nano could barely disguise the shake in her voice. 'She deserves better than this at her age!'

Mary-Brigid hugged her aunt close, smelling her usual scent of lavender water.

'Mrs O'Brien, please collect your things and leave this dwelling,' ordered the younger constable, ignoring Nano's plea. 'No one wants to hurt you or harm you; we want to keep this as peaceable as possible.'

The older constable looked around him at the swelling crowd. People were sitting on the low stone wall, leaning against the rusty gate, standing in the overgrown patch of garden. The last thing he wanted was for a mob situation to develop.

He knew a lot of the people here. By and large they were mostly good folk. He himself felt uncomfortable at having to enforce an eviction order against an elderly woman all alone.

'Do something, constable,' muttered the bailiff.

'All in good time,' replied the older constable. He was not going to provoke a situation unless he had to.

'Oh poor Agnes! That poor woman! Perhaps if I went

in and talked to her,' Nano said quietly to Eily. 'I'm afraid she'll get injured or hurt during this.'

Nano pushed her way to the door of the cottage. 'Agnes, dear!' she called out. 'It's Nano Murphy. Do you want me to come in and give you a hand? I know what's running through your mind at this moment, but believe me when I tell you, you have many friends and neighbours here with you.'

Agnes was obviously at the other side of the door, listening. 'Ye may come in, Nano,' she whispered.

Eily grabbed at her elderly aunt. 'Nano, I'm coming with you,' she whispered frantically. 'What if Agnes locks you in there with her?'

Nano frowned for a second, then shook her head as they heard the rusty latch lift. 'Don't you worry, Eily, you stay with the children! Remember, Agnes and I are friends. She wouldn't harm me.'

Mary-Brigid felt as if her heart would stop beating. She was not going to let Nano go inside on her own. She darted quickly behind Nano's long, full, black skirt and shawl, and followed her in.

'I'll only be a few minutes,' Nano called to the bailiff.

The bailiff tried to shove past the crowd but the constable blocked his way. 'Let her be,' he ordered.

Nano pushed in the door to the damp, smoky room. Agnes was standing in the middle of it all, a small, slight, scrawny figure in a grey shift, her hair hanging in streaks around her pale, anxious face.

'What am I going to do, Nano?' she whispered. 'Where am I going to go?'

Mary-Brigid wrinkled her nose. The room was dirty and smelly and untidy, the fire nothing more than soft ash. There was barely a stick of furniture in the place and the few bits of crockery the woman had lay dirty in the sink or on the small kitchen table.

Nano turned around and saw her. 'How did you get in here, Mary-Brigid? You never listen to a word I say, child. I'm scalded with you!' Mary-Brigid tried to look downcast and ashamed, but she was glad to be there with Nano. 'Still, you've a good heart! Hasn't she Agnes?' Nano added.

'Aye!' whispered the old lady, who was now crouched on the narrow, iron bed which stood against the wall.

'Agnes, girl, the time has come to leave this place. I know you're broken-hearted, but they'll not let you stop here any longer. You must gather your things and your clothes. Pack up now,' urged Nano.

'I'll not go!' screeched the old woman. 'Let them burn me out if they want. I'm willing to die.'

'Hush, Agnes, none of that kind of talk. You'll not let them destroy you. You'll walk out of here with your head held high.'

Mary-Brigid thought it far more likely that Agnes would be dragged out the door kicking and screaming and cursing.

'Mary-Brigid,' ordered Nano, 'see if there is any warm water left in that kettle over there. The ware in the sink could do with a bit of a wash, no doubt, then we'll dry it and wrap it up.

'You must have a dress and a pair of boots, Agnes,' she continued. 'Come on, now, and we'll get you dressed.'

The distressed woman pointed to a worn, dark navy, wool dress hanging from a hook behind the door. Nano fetched it, shaking it before she pulled it over the unprotesting figure sitting on the edge of the unmade bed. The near-threadbare grey stockings and mud-spattered boots lay flung underneath the bed. Nano watched as the widow squeezed her bony, gnarled toes into the stockings.

'That's a lot better!' stated Nano, talking the way you would to cajole a small child like Jodie.

Nano dragged the cleanest of the grimy-looking woollen blankets off the bed and laid the rest of the old lady's clothes in it. 'Mary-Brigid, you can help by gathering up some of Agnes's bits and pieces.' Mary-Brigid was pleased to leave the washing-up to Nano as the greasy plates, encrusted with stale food, had almost turned her stomach. She looked around the room. There was a small, torn bible, and a carved crucifix that hung over the bed. There were a few shabby ornaments and some chipped bowls. That was what remained of Agnes's family life.

Nano poured warm water over the rest of the crockery and the two or three items of glass that Mrs O'Brien possessed, then she dried them off as quickly as she could.

'Agnes,' Nano said gently, 'tell me, which are the special keepsakes you want wrapped carefully?'

The bent, arthritic fingers pointed out two favourite cups and saucers, then a willow-pattern serving plate and a matching bowl and three drinking glasses. Nano wrapped them all carefully in the sheet Mary-Brigid passed to her, hoping they wouldn't break.

'Smash that door down, man!' ordered the bailiff. 'She's had more than enough time already!' Mary-Brigid jumped as the glass in the window shattered and the bailiff's ugly face peered into the room.

'A few more minutes, constable, please,' pleaded Nano. 'We're almost ready!'

She offered her own dampened handkerchief to Agnes, telling her to wipe her face and freshen herself up. 'Have you a brush, Agnes, a hairbrush? We'll tidy your hair up.'

Mary-Brigid watched, amazed, as Nano calmly brushed the greasy grey streaks of hair back and upwards into a tidy bun. 'Have you any hair pins, Agnes?' The other woman, who seemed almost in a daze, pointed forlornly to the rickety chair near the bed. Nano tidied her hair up securely. 'Are ye nearly ready, Agnes, do you think?'

The commotion outside was getting worse. Agnes O'Brien stood up. Her eyes scanned the small, familiar room, a shudder going through her at the thought of leaving it. Mary-Brigid half-expected her to pull the pins from her hair and drag off the dress and curl up by the ashes. Instead, she wrapped the thin grey shawl she took from behind the door tightly around her.

'Good times and bad times I've had under this roof,' Agnes whispered, 'but I never imagined it ending like this.' Tears ran down her cheeks as Nano escorted her out into the sunlight. Eily ran from the crowd and helped Mary-Brigid lift out the parcelled-up blanket and the sheet-wrapped crockery.

The crowd stood hushed, as the Widow O'Brien left her cottage for the last time. Then, one by one, the neighbours began to file past her, each offering her their condolences and wishing her well in the future.

The bailiff strode by them all into the low cottage, and was amazed to find so few possessions.

'You'll hold on there, sir!' warned the older constable. 'We wouldn't want you to damage any of the lady's valuables.'

'Valuables!' jeered the bailiff. 'There's nothing of value here.'

Dermot O'Reilly, who lived about two miles down the road, had arrived with a donkey and cart. 'Mrs O'Brien, if you give the say-so, I'll put whatever you want on the cart and I'll be pleased to drop you wherever you wish.'

Mary-Brigid watched as they loaded the few bits and pieces up.

'Will ye not come home for a sup of tea and a piece of bread with us, Agnes?' pleaded Nano. 'You wouldn't mind, Eily, sure you wouldn't?'

''Tis all right, Nano. You've done more than enough,' murmured the poor widow woman before Eily had a chance to speak. 'I'm best to get into the town to try and find somewhere to stay.' She raised her voice. 'They can tumble my cottage, tear it down stone by stone, but they can't take away the fact that me and mine lived and died here. I have two sons and, would you believe it, eight grandchildren. The O'Briens will always be a part of this place. No-one can change that!'

Nano stood proudly as her old friend turned to her neighbours and friends and said goodbye. The crowd all watched her climb onto the cart and set off over the rough ground to the roadway, her face almost see-through, the thin shawl wrapped around her head and shoulders.

'What will happen to her now, Mammy? Where will she go?' sobbed Mary-Brigid, hot tears stinging her face and throat.

'I'm not sure, pet. The sons might send her some money and maybe she'll rent a room someplace, or she'll get a place in the Union home for the destitute!' murmured Eily sadly. 'To tell the truth, Mary-Brigid, I don't rightly know!'

'It's not fair! They shouldn't have done it!' shouted Mary-Brigid, anger burning in her young heart. She knew that she would never forget this terrible day.

CHAPTER 8

The Races

DAWN WAS BREAKING when Michael and the rest of the stable lads roused themselves. Race days always meant an early start. There were all the normal chores to be done – mucking out, the early-morning ride-out which gave the horses a chance to gallop and warm up for the day ahead – as well as getting the chosen horses ready, grooming them till their coats shone and checking that all their tack was in perfect condition.

Glengarry and Morning Boy stood lazily watching the goings-on from the small fenced enclosure for young foals. The colt was growing steadier on his feet and gaining weight. He was beginning to look healthier week by week. His ears pricked up as he watched the other racehorses prepare to head off. Michael was almost reluctant to leave the stables and the small colt.

'Promise me you'll take good care of Morning Boy,' he begged young Brendan.

'You know I will,' replied the stable lad, aware of his friend's concern.

'Make sure that the mare doesn't nip or bite at him. You know a mare can turn on a foal in an instant.'

''Tis all right, Michael, I promise you I'll look after the two of them.'

'Michael O'Driscoll, will you get up on that horse and stop holding us up,' teased Toss. The rest of the jockeys were ready, and were getting impatient waiting for him.

'Make sure he's feeding properly!' Michael shouted.

He grabbed hold of the front of his saddle and pulled himself up onto Nero, and as soon as he was mounted they all clip-clopped out across the cobbled yard. It was always nerve-racking, setting off to the races. It was only then that you realised how good or bad the horses really were.

The lads and grooms who were staying behind stopped what they were doing to wish them well.

'Good luck to ye all!'

'Let's hope ye have a winner!'

Michael had eaten very little for breakfast, in fact he'd gone soft on the food for the last few days trying to keep the weight off. His fellow jockey, Liam Quigley, was as small and light as a leprechaun and had no bother keeping to the right size, but Michael was a whole lot taller and with his wide shoulders and strong build, he was a bit heavier than most jockeys. Still, Nero was a big horse and he reckoned that was why Toss and Lord Henry had said he should ride him.

Peadar Mahoney was riding in front of Michael. As usual, he held Jerpoint tight at the bit with a short rein. The lively black horse snorted angrily at being so restrained and tossed his head frantically.

Toss was out in front of them all, lost in thought, as he led the party across the dew-soaked fields at a gentle gallop.

It was late afternoon by the time they arrived at Killross, horses and riders equally weary and glad to rest. The animals were watered and fed. Nero munched at the sweet, juicy hay that Michael hung from the rack in his stall. Nearby, the racecourse lay flat and wide in the distance, ready for the next day's excitement.

Though Peadar and Liam tried to persuade him to join them for a stroll up the town, Michael decided to stay with Nero. He would enjoy just as well sitting listening to the stories of past races and exploits that the riders shared with each other as the evening drew in.

Mercy Farrell, the young housemaid, had insisted he take a small package from her. Opening his bag, Michael discovered a portion of white chicken meat, some cold potato, a scone and a piece of some kind of pie – he tested it with his finger: 'twas apple.

Mercy had him spoiled. He only had to appear at the kitchen door to see how she was getting on and she'd have him sitting at the table, stuffing him with food as she chattered on, the cook watching them. Cook wouldn't tolerate any lovey-dovey stuff in her kitchen, but she couldn't help but think that Michael O'Driscoll and young Mercy Farrell made a lovely couple. Michael put the apple-tart aside – he'd save it till after his race, but the rest he'd eat now. He was hungry after the journey. Tonight he'd sleep in the stall with Nero. No-one would tamper with any of the Buckland horses while he was around.

Race day itself was good and dry with a nice bit of a breeze for racing. Michael's stomach was wound in a knot of apprehension as he prepared himself for the afternoon event.

The small racecourse had started to fill up, the gentlemen and their visitors filing in to watch the spectacle. The gentlemen were clad in top-hats and fine jackets and they eyed the competition and considered the odds carefully before placing their bets.

Michael weighed in on the large scales before joining the lads that were in his race. There were eight runners. He smiled over at Ned Mangan and Tod O'Sullivan – they'd all raced against one another before.

Nero quivered with excitement as they passed down by the crowds. 'Good boy,' said Michael, patting the horse's neck and shortening his stirrups a fraction more.

Michael cantered Nero slowly down to the starting line. He had spotted Lord Henry in the distance, standing with a group of other gentlemen.

'Best horse wins!' shouted Tod O'Sullivan, his skinny face all eager and excited.

Nero pranced about, itching to be off. Michael sat in the saddle, tense and alert, waiting for the signal.

They were away! Tod O'Sullivan's horse took off like the wind, its swinging reddish tail out in front, taunting them all. Michael had to hold Nero steady, a burst of pace now would be too soon. He lifted himself off the saddle as speed surged through the horse.

'Keep it steady, Nero!' He could sense the racehorse getting into a strong, even stride as he raced forwards, arching his neck. Nero tightened the gap between himself and Tod O'Sullivan's horse. Closer ... closer ... until he passed him out!

The grass seemed to race beneath Michael and even

the clouds that blew across the wide blue sky could
not keep up with him. His heart was beating fast, just
the way the horse's was. At this moment they were one,
racing together.

At his shoulder he caught a flicker of colour – Tod
and some of the other lads were creeping up on him.
He urged Nero on, faster, faster ... the horse's powerful
legs flew through the air, thundering against the earth.
Then Tod's horse pushed itself on again, breathing
heavily with the effort. Nero swung his full weight
forward, trying to outdo the other. The blood coursed
and pumped through Michael's head and veins and
ears as he pushed Nero as hard as he could. It made
no difference. Tod's horse pulled across the finishing
line a second or two ahead of him.

'Well done!' he called to Tod, trying to swallow his
bitter disappointment.

'Tough luck!' shouted Tod. 'That horse of yours gave
us a right chase!'

Michael watched as the winner was applauded. He
jumped down off Nero as soon as he saw Lord Henry
and Toss appearing.

'Well done, lad,' smiled Toss. 'You ran a great race!'

'But I didn't win,' moaned Michael.

'You did your best, Michael,' said Lord Henry. 'Nero
will win sooner or later.'

Michael ran his fingers through his sweat-soaked hair, glad that neither man was annoyed with him. He decided to rub Nero down and then come back to watch how Liam and Peadar got on in their races.

Liam romped home on Troy, waving to Michael and the crowd, his small face creased with a huge grin.

Jerpoint was acting up a bit, and Michael had a job holding her still as Peadar tried to mount her. The young jockey was annoyed as he galloped her down to the starting line where the other five entrants were waiting patiently. Lord Henry and his friends had put a large wager on her to win.

Peadar's face was taut as he waited for the race to start. He still held the horse far too tight for Michael's liking.

From the very first second Jerpoint was out in front, pushing ahead of the others, her jet-black mane flying. Peadar was using his stick like a madman, hitting her on, as the rest of the field tried to catch them. The horse was terrified and as they came more into his view, Michael knew that the mare was simply running her heart out to get away from the madman on her back. She crossed the line four lengths ahead of the rest of the field, and the spectators went wild.

Gentlemen came up immediately to clap Lord Henry on the back and congratulate him on his excellent win.

A huge smile lit up Peadar's long, gawky face as he savoured his moment of triumph. The horse was panting and shivering, the long welts on her flank showing like stripes against her sweaty coat, foam dripping from her mouth.

'Get off that horse!' ordered Toss, handing Jerpoint's rein to Michael. 'You look after her, lad,' he ordered, following Peadar towards the presentation of prizes.

Later, they all rode home in silence, Toss and Michael out in front. Jerpoint was being led on a halter-lead. She wasn't fit to be ridden.

'Are ye disappointed about coming second, Michael?' asked Toss.

Michael thought about it. 'Nah! Not really, Toss. Tod's horse was very good and he's ridden in far more races than I have. He's a good jockey.'

'More than I can say for some,' muttered Toss.

'Tod's horse is a brother of Ragusa.'

'Is that so?' enquired Toss.

'That means the same bloodline as Morning Boy,' added Michael knowledgeably.

'You're learning!' chuckled Toss.

Michael nodded. Toss had talked to him day in, day out about the importance of bloodline in a good horse. You could tell more about a horse by learning its family tree than by watching it race.

Toss reckoned the Irish horse was the best in the world, strong and steady and with a heart as big as Galway Bay itself, wherever that was. Long ago, the bloodline of the best of Irish horses had been crossed with a strong Arab horse which had charged into the battle of the Boyne – the Byerly Turk had passed on his courage to his progeny, creating a bloodline that passed through many of the colts and fillies that Toss would in time train.

'You're a good lad, Michael, and the horses know it,' murmured Toss.

Michael could feel the happiness swelling inside him. He was itching to see Morning Boy and to tell Mercy about his race. He knew the kind-hearted girl would hug him even more when she heard that Nero and himself were the runners-up.

* * *

'I've had more than enough of you, my lad!' Michael heard the anger in Toss's voice. It was the day after the races and he was busy polishing some of the tack in preparation for the early ride-out when Toss and Peadar Mahoney walked through the door of the harness room. 'Careless! Stupid! Cruel! That's what I'd call it.'

'It's only a damned horse!' came Peadar's smart reply.

'Look, my lad, you'd better begin to understand
– these horses are our bread-and-butter. The other men
hereabouts have to break the ground and till the fields
and tend the sheep and do all sorts of labour for his
lordship. We're lucky. We are the ones responsible for
his horses.'

'I'm the best jockey he's got, you know that, Toss!'
shouted Peadar angrily.

'That don't give you no right to treat a pure-bred
horse like that. It's not a carthorse, ye know. Them
horses cost a fortune. You should see the bills for their
feed.'

Michael could see Peadar shrugging his shoulders.
He didn't care that he had over-ridden Jerpoint. He'd
won, hadn't he? The racehorse was still in a desperate
state but Peadar seemed to think that all the rules for
caring for a horse could be broken and it didn't
matter.

'I'm not about to sit back and let you destroy a good
horse,' said Toss, 'because that's what's going to happen.'

'I'll run good races, win all around me. In time I'll
win in the Curragh,' jeered the young jockey. 'I'll win
in England, too,' he added. 'I'll make his lordship a
fortune. A racehorse needs a firm hand!'

'It don't make a difference if you're the best jockey in the whole of Ireland, the horse is the thing. You have to care for the horse. I can't have anybody around this yard that don't understand the value of these horses. I won't have them, and Lord Henry agrees with me.'

'Lord Henry!'

'Aye! He saw Jerpoint this morning.'

'What would he know about it?' shrugged Peadar.

'More than you think. I've instructions to give you your marching orders,' said Toss firmly. 'How and ever, I'm giving you one last chance. But one more misdeed and you're finished here at Castletaggart, my lad!'

Peadar stood for a second, stunned, his greasy, brown hair falling over his eyes.

'And for the moment you'll look after the rest of the horses,' continued Toss. 'The other lads will attend to the racers and you'll do no riding-out. And, by the way, you'll be the one to muck out Jerpoint's stable while she's resting up.'

Without a word, Peadar turned on his heel and left the tack room.

Michael coughed.

'You heard?' asked Toss uneasily. Michael nodded. 'The lad's a good rider but he has a lot to learn about horses, else he's no use to us.' With that, Toss took down one of the leather saddles and left.

Michael loved the early-morning ride-out; it was the time that he treasured most in the whole day. The horses were fresh and itching to gallop, the chilly morning air turning their breath to clouds. Each race-horse had a different temperament, all needing a different approach – some gentle coaxing and patting, others a sharp hand.

It was only when Michael checked in on Jerpoint later that he wondered about Peadar. The horse was standing in a fresh pile of dung – why the hell hadn't Peadar attended to her? He searched around the stables and out by the paddocks, but there wasn't sight nor sign of him.

Michael climbed up to the sleeping quarters above the coach-house and looked in the corner that Peadar had made his own. Peadar's blanket was still there, but there was no sign of any of his clothes or boots or his few personal bits and pieces. He's done a runner, thought Michael to himself.

'Has Mr Know-It-All taken himself off?' Brendan had followed Michael up to the room.

Michael shrugged. 'It looks like it.'

'I'd heard that Toss gave out to him this morning. Good riddance is what I say.' The young stableboy smirked; he had so often got a clatter from Peadar for no reason. 'Nobody's going to miss the likes of Peadar.'

'Yeh, I suppose so,' agreed Michael, though secretly he was sure they hadn't heard the last of Peadar Mahoney, not by a long shot!

CHAPTER 9

Harvest Home

THE SUN BLAZED BRIGHTLY day after day through the late summer as every man, woman and child old enough to help worked on bringing in the harvest. Even the horses seemed to pick up the air of excitement and cantered across the fields to see what was going on. Women and youngsters carried cans of milk and thick cuts of bread to the men who worked at saving the hay till the sweat dripped off them.

The carts were piled as high as could be with the sweet-smelling hay, the horses straining to pull them. Stooks of wheat were tied, ready for thrashing, and oats and barley stored in huge cereal bins. The work continued on long into the summer evenings, till the exhausted workers finally went home at sunset to sleep.

Michael unharnessed and patted the big old farm-horses who were now the heroes – they well deserved their tin buckets full of oats and the respect of those who worked with them on the estate.

''Tis a grand harvest,' said Brendan.

'Better than last year even,' agreed Michael.

'Lord Henry will be rightly pleased.'

Brendan nudged Michael and pointed at Markey, the donkey, who trotted past them pulling a small cart. 'I see they even have Markey working hard. 'Tis about time!'

Michael chuckled. The donkey's only job in recent years had been to keep the racehorses company. Any of them that got lonely or seemed to be acting up always improved if they had the old grey donkey to share their field or paddock with them.

Rolling up their sleeves and pulling on their caps, Michael and Brendan ran to help unload Markey's cart.

Michael could remember a time long ago when he was only a small boy helping his father, bending low to pick up stray blades of wheat scattered on the ground. He could almost see the curly, dark head, as black as his own, the powerful shoulders, the sweat-soaked shirt clinging to the muscles, and then the laughing voices of his mother and two sisters, Eily and Peggy, as they ran across the fields with a jug of cold,

cold water from the well and boiled potatoes wrapped in a cloth and still warm from the pot in their home at Duneen.

'Are ye all right, Michael?' enquired Brendan, looking anxiously at his friend who had suddenly stopped working.

'The sun is blinding me, that's all,' said Michael softly, unwilling to banish the childhood memory and the comfort it gave him.

Finally, one night as the sun sank and the fields lay trim and gleaming, the field-mouse scurrying to find her lost mate, the corncrake safe with her young in a small uncut patch, the host of small birds fighting over the feast, it was time for the workers to be rewarded.

The kitchen staff had been busy for days and the whitewashed laundry rooms had been cleaned. Huge trestle tables were set up for the harvest supper. There were roasted meats and huge bowls of floury potatoes, trays full of griddle cakes and oat biscuits, jugs of thick brown gravy and boiled carrots and baby cabbages they called sprouts.

Michael ate and ate, his stomach so full in the end he felt it would surely burst. Mercy laughed at him, as she avoided the glances of the farmers' sons, her eyes twinkling only at him. Outside there were barrels of porter and ale and a punchbowl for the womenfolk and lemonade for the children. Lord Henry and his wife, Martha, joined them all, dressed in their finery, while their daughters, Rose and Felicia, in matching pink dresses, giggled with excitement as they took in the scene and mingled with the tenants. Felicia spotted Michael and made him shove up on his bench so she could sit beside him. She gabbled on about the high jinks they were having and pointed out her cousins, and her uncle Robert who was home from India.

The empty coach-house was soon filled with the sound of the fiddle and pipes as Dermot and Dinny Callaghan, two old bachelors who lived down by the river, began to play.

Old men and young men alike twirled the women around the room, dancing to their hearts' content. Michael grabbed hold of Mercy, never letting go of her hand for a minute the whole night long. 'Isn't it grand!' she laughed as they danced together, keeping in step with the lively music. After a while the coach-house became too hot and crowded, so like many of the younger folk they found themselves dancing out under the stars. Mercy uncoiled her thick plait of wavy brown hair, letting it tumble around her shoulders as she waltzed with Michael O'Driscoll, the boy she loved.

It was late by the time the Callaghans stopped playing and the company began to break up. Farmers lifted sleepy children onto their shoulders and mothers wrapped their shawls around themselves as they made their way back home across the fields. Michael fell onto his bed, muscles aching, heart pounding, the horses quiet below.

CHAPTER 10

Lonesome Times

 MRS ELIZABETH ROWAN WAS UPSET. She wept as she said goodbye to her now-married daughter, and waved sadly as Roxanne and Fletcher's carriage turned in the driveway and headed out through the open gates, leaving Rushton behind.

'I don't think I can bear it, Peggy, I miss her so much already,' she said as Peggy poured her a cup of coffee, the rich brown liquid filling the white china cup.

'I understand how you feel, Ma'am,' said Peggy shyly.

Kitty had gone on ahead of her new mistress, escorting the wedding gifts and some special pieces of furniture from her home that Roxanne's parents had insisted she keep. Peggy was feeling mighty lonesome herself, now that her best friend had gone.

'The best thing is to keep busy, visit people, visit new places, that's what my friends have told me. Perhaps my husband and I will go and visit Roxanne when she's settled.'

'I'm sure she'd love that, Ma'am. It'd be a chance for you to see her house and get to know Baltimore a bit better.'

'Yes, indeed!' Mrs Rowan sipped the coffee daintily. 'We'll give her time to settle in though.'

There was a fruit tart and a tray of honey biscuits baking in the oven. Mrs O'Connor was relieved that the fuss and flurry of the wedding was over and that things had returned to normal, at least in the kitchen. Of course, the mistress wasn't herself – all broody and tense and tearful and barely eating a pick, no matter how fine a meal was served up to her.

And as for Peggy O'Driscoll – it was as if the young maid had had her left arm cut off! She no longer sang or hummed as she went about her work. At night she would sit in the kitchen curled up reading a book, joining in conversation only when Mrs O'Connor or Eliza Whitman deliberately asked her a question.

Mrs O'Connor was anxious about Peggy. The departure of her friend had taken all the spark out of the girl. They would replace that young one Kitty eventually, of course, but that might take time. Peggy was due a day off, thought Mrs O'Connor, perhaps that would cheer her up a bit. She could visit some of her Irish friends; it might put a bit of colour back in her cheeks and sparkle in her eyes.

* * *

Peggy strode along Russell Avenue. The sun beat down on her back and on her straw bonnet. The heat of the pavement seeped up through the light shoe-leather. It was another scorcher. The sky above her was blue and cloudless. Back home when she was young, herself and her big sister Eily used to lie on the grass in their field and make pictures out of the clouds, telling each other stories, as the soft white shapes rolled across the sky above them. But here the summer sky was cruel, the sun blazing down relentlessly.

Peggy crossed the narrow street and made her way to the dreary entrance of the apartment building where Sarah lived with her two brothers. She climbed the depressing, dirty stairs, hitching up her skirt so as to avoid the dust and peeling plasterwork.

Sarah's landing was clean and swept, and the linoleum washed. The long, narrow window was open and the glass – well, as far as Sarah could reach – was polished. Peggy knocked on the door. Sarah's brother, John, opened it and smiled warmly when he saw her.

'It's Peggy, Sarah!' he called.

'I'll be out in a second, Peggy, sit ye down. I'm just finishing getting dressed.'

Peggy sat on the round, squashy armchair. A mauve throw-over covered it in a vain attempt to disguise the ripped arm where the stuffing protruded. Looking around the large room, Peggy guessed that Sarah had been up since early morning, tidying. The clothes rail had been folded away and the circular table covered with a lace tablecloth and set with the assorted mismatch of crockery that her friend possessed. A row of cheerful blue and yellow cushions rested on the grey velvet couch the brothers had bought in the second-hand market three years ago. There was a multicoloured rug on the floor and a basket of lavender was propped in front of the fireplace.

'Would you like a cup of tea, Peggy, while you're waiting?' enquired John.

Peggy nodded. She watched as he set the kettle to boil on the small stove and searched for a clean spoon.

Sarah came out of the bedroom, and ran to embrace Peggy. 'Oh, Peggy it's grand to see you! Tell me all the news. I'm dying to hear all about the wedding and Miss Roxanne.'

Sarah looked tired. There were smudges of grey under her eyes and her skin had a pale, translucent sheen to it. Peggy couldn't help but notice her friend's broken nails and bruised fingers, and she saw that Sarah held one hand stiffly and that it looked very sore.

Sarah bit her lip. 'Don't say it, Peggy! I had to do a few more days' button-work. The other girl was sick.'

'But, Sarah, your poor hands!'

Peggy didn't know how Sarah stuck working in Goldman's shirt factory. The hours were long and the work tedious, although the wages were higher than Peggy's. The button-work cracked her nails and tore her skin and left zig-zag scars and weals on her fingers. Her hands were often left rigid and swollen and practically unusable for days. Sarah had tried some of the other machines, but the fibres and dust that flew from the raw materials made her eyes and nose water and gave her a constant cough.

Sarah had gone for a few job interviews, but one look at her hands made sure there would be no offer of other employment. Peggy had pleaded with her to wear gloves to these interviews, but Sarah had said that that would be dishonest, and so she had remained at Goldman's.

'I brought fruit cake for ye and a few biscuits,' Peggy said, changing the subject so as not to upset Sarah – Mrs O'Connor had made her take one of the rich left-over fruitcakes to her friend.

'That's very kind of you, thank you, Peggy,' murmured Sarah, her eyes soft and gentle.

'Thank Mrs O'Connor,' said Peggy, taking a sip of the tea.

'Will I cut some of the cake now?' enquired Sarah.

'Not for me! I'm sick of all that stuff left over after the wedding,' said Peggy. 'Save it for yourselves later.'

'Very well, for when we're having our meal. It's a lovely day outside, Peggy, will we take a stroll in the sun?'

Peggy was about to say no, not in the blistering heat, when she realised that Sarah badly needed a few hours away from this building and street. 'Aye! It's grand outside. Come on.'

Sarah fetched her best shawl and Peggy made her put on her lightest bonnet. John smiled at the two of them as they went off in high spirits. Linking arms, the girls made their way downstairs and out into the bright daylight of the street.

'Let's go to the Common!' suggested Peggy. It was one of her favourite places in Boston.

There were crowds of people walking – families, fine gentlemen and their good wives, romantic sweethearts. Peggy and Sarah walked amongst them all. In the distance a band played, the lively tune drifting through the air. Peggy and Sarah giggled as two groups of young men lifted their hats to them and tried to engage them in conversation. There wasn't an empty park-bench in sight, so the two of them sat on a patch of grass in the dappled sunlight under the shade of an elm tree.

Sarah was breathless after the walk and was trying to cough discreetly into her handkerchief.

'Are you feeling unwell?' enquired Peggy.

The other girl stopped, as if considering, and stared into the distance where swan-shaped boats were gliding silently across the lake. 'Actually, Peggy, I went to Doctor O'Connor down near the factory. James and John made me go. They said that they were fed up of my being sick.'

'What did he say?'

'Well ... he said he wouldn't recommend me to continue on working at the factory. He said the fibres and dust were giving me lung infections ...' she trailed off.

'What'll you do?'

'James and John have great plans. They want to leave the city. They have both saved money from their wages and they think the time is right now for them to purchase land and stake the Connolly claim.'

'What do you mean?'

'They want to join one of those wagon trains heading

out west, and they want me to go with them!'

Peggy let out a gasp of amazement. 'You wouldn't go, Sarah, would you?'

'That's just it, Peggy, I will! I don't want to stay here in Boston without my brothers. It's all right for you – you have Kitty and the Rowans and Miss Whitman and Mrs O'Connor to share everything with. If James and John go, I'll have nobody!'

Peggy sat very still. A wobbly heat-haze seemed to have made the people on the path and around her shimmer, their voices coming and going.

'Peggy! Peggy!' Sarah gripped her friend's arm, excitement lighting up her eyes. 'I wish you'd come with us! James and John said there would be space for you. We could all share the work and ...' But Sarah stopped. Peggy didn't seem to be listening. Obviously, it was not to be.

Peggy tried to collect herself. There was no point in telling Sarah that Kitty had gone and how lonesome she felt already. Sarah's health was breaking down, it was only sensible for herself and the brothers to go in search of a place of their own. She herself would carry on working – polishing and washing and cleaning and pressing clothes and helping Mrs O'Connor serve meal after meal. She was just a maid and that was her station in life. She had a good job and was earning good money.

Every month the bank collector called to the back-kitchen door and she would give him another small deposit from her wages. Mr Keane would sit at the kitchen table and fill in the amount in the small black bank-book she kept hidden under her mattress. He would stamp it with the mark of the East Coast Savings Bank before joining herself and the rest of the staff who saved with him for a cup of tea and a chat. Usually, he would tell them that business was booming and how their money was growing and accumulating. It did her good to listen to him. When he was gone she would run her eyes up and down the columns of figures, mentally totting up her savings. This was her independence.

Peggy came back to the present. The mid-west was so far away – some people called it the wild west. Oh why did Sarah have to go so far away?

'Peggy,' said the other girl, tapping her shoulder. 'What do you think?'

To be honest, Peggy didn't know what to think, but when she looked into Sarah's pinched, white face and thought of the factory where tomorrow she would spend every daylight hour working, Peggy knew that leaving the city and moving into the open countryside would mean salvation for Sarah, and a fresh start.

'I think it's grand, Sarah! Honestly I do,' said Peggy

hugging her friend, 'and by the time you all get settled, they'll have built the railroads and I'll keep on saving every dollar and dime and in no time I'll have enough money to come and visit you.'

Sarah clapped her hands softly. 'Oh Peggy! That would be great. But I'll really miss you. I do wish you would come with us.'

The rest of that sunny afternoon was spent strolling through different parts of the park, chatting and laughing and giggling. Peggy gave Sarah a blow-by-blow account of Roxanne's wedding and Sarah told her all the latest gossip of the factory. They watched as a group of young men played football together. They counted the growing young ducks and cygnets on the lake, and admired the latest styles worn by fashionable ladies who promenaded with their parasols.

'Come on, Peggy! We must go home and get something to eat,' urged Sarah finally, adjusting her bonnet.

With great reluctance, Peggy stood up from the park bench where they were sitting, realising that this was probably the very last time that she would spend her day off with her friend.

Sarah busied herself cooking a meal once they got back to the apartment. James and John were both there, and they were full of excitement telling Peggy of their future plans.

'We've enough put by to buy acres and acres,' said James proudly, 'and, God willing, John and I will build a fine house of wood for all of us.'

'We'll have to clear the land, break the soil. It'll all be new,' John joined in. 'Imagine, Peggy, we won't be tenants like we'd be back home, we'll own our own land. What we claim will be ours! This is surely a great land of opportunity for Irishmen and Irishwomen.'

Peggy helped Sarah drain the potatoes and slice the boiled beef. Then they all pulled up their chairs, and said Grace before they began to eat.

The food was good but Peggy couldn't eat. She tried to smile as she listened to all the exciting plans.

'When are you going?' she asked finally.

The others were silent for a few seconds.

'We have things to organise,' James explained. 'Horses and a wagon to buy, business to wind up here, but all going well we plan to leave within the next two to three weeks. We must go while the weather is good so we'll be settled by winter.'

They talked on and on for hours. Peggy was very reluctant to leave, aware that she could not guarantee another Sunday off before they departed. But Sarah was getting sleepy, her eyes closing heavily.

'Sarah! You must go to bed,' said John. 'You've a long day's work tomorrow.'

'Oh, I'm sorry,' sighed Sarah. 'I'm such bad company. At the moment I seem to be tired and sleepy all the time.'

Peggy stood up. 'I should be getting back to Rushton. I've stayed far too late.' She tried to hide the sadness in her voice. 'I'd best be going, Sarah, I have a long walk home. Luckily, it's a grand night.'

'When will I see you again?' asked her friend.

Peggy considered. 'I'm not sure, but I'll be bound to get an hour or two off or a half-day soon. I'll come and see you before you go, I promise.'

As she bade them goodbye, she noticed that James had disappeared. She was surprised to find him waiting below, outside on the street, with the delivery cart he and John used for work and one of the horses.

'Let me drive you home, Peggy!' he said, helping her up on the front seat beside him.

They drove through the almost deserted city. James was silent, lost in his own thoughts. He was the quieter of the two brothers, more serious and reserved than John. As they drove through the dark countryside he began to tell Peggy about his dreams of the prairies and plains, of the rolling blue skies, of fields of wheat and corn, of the herds of buffalo and of the log cabin they would build. 'There'll be a polished wood floor and a kitchen where the sun will shine through all day long,' he said excitedly, 'and a stove for cooking and warmth, and store cupboards to hold provisions that will last for months – they say the winters are hard there and you can be snowed in – and a fine, big, solid, wooden table for family and folks to sit and eat and talk at.'

'It sounds lovely,' said Peggy dreamily.

'Come winter, there'll be a blazing log fire and some comfortable chairs close by, and a table to hold a lamp and shelves for books.'

He had slowed the horse down so it was almost walking. Peggy could feel his grey-blue eyes staring at her – lucky it was too dark for him to notice her blush. James was handsome, with a narrow face and kind eyes. His hair was jet black like Sarah's, and always seemed to need a trim. He was tall and rangy and kind of clumsy. He was a hard worker, his hands rough and calloused from heavy labouring. She had known him since they had sailed on the *Fortunata* from Queenstown over six years ago. He'd always been around. They'd gone to mass together, talked about the old days back in Ireland, strolled around Boston, had snowball fights and skated on the river in the cold winters, danced a jig in the front room of Mrs Byrne's at the *céilí* – he was, after all, Sarah's brother, and a friend.

'Peggy ...' he said, 'Peggy, I want to ask you something.'

Peggy lifted her eyes to meet his gaze.

'Will you come with us?' he asked suddenly. 'Come with me, I mean? I need a partner.'

She let out a wobbly kind of gasp.

'Will you marry me, Peggy, be my wife?'

Peggy didn't know what to say. James was actually proposing to her. She couldn't believe it!

'You and Sarah are close friends. You'd be companions for each other. We would all be able to help each other to build a new life out west.'

Peggy closed her eyes. He only wanted a partner, someone to help plant the corn and feed the cattle and cook the meals. That's all it was. He was just used to her, to having her around.

'What do you think, Peggy?' he said reaching for her hand.

'James! I don't know. I was talking to Sarah earlier. I told her that when you're all settled, maybe the railroad will have reached wherever you have gone to, and I would just love to come and visit you ...'

He held her hand, squeezing it gently. 'I'm rushing you. I suppose it's not fair to just spring it on you like this, especially when we're leaving so soon ...'

The night air was heavy and still, the closeness wrapping itself around Peggy, the scent of magnolia and jasmines escaping from the gardens they drove past. It all made her feel almost dizzy as the cart bumped along the narrow laneways.

James slipped his arm around her and she sat rigid, trying to resist the temptation to snuggle close to him while they jostled along. She was lost in a storm of confusion as they came in sight of Rushton.

They came to a halt near the large gateway. The driveway and hedges gleamed in the moonlight. He sat silent, waiting for her answer.

'Home sweet home,' he said, smiling.

'James, I am very honoured by you asking me ... by your proposal ... I don't know what to say. You know I would love to be with the three of you, stay part of your lives. It's just that ...' she whispered feebly, 'I have my job and my life here,' she said gesticulating wildly at the large house.

'I see,' said James politely.

Peggy sat, miserable. She didn't want to leave him like this. 'Can't we be friends, James, and I promise to come and visit you ...'

'Friends it is then,' he replied stiffly.

Suddenly he leaned forward and, catching her unawares, tilted up her chin and kissed her. Her mind told her to pull away but instead she savoured the warmth of his full lips and soft breath against her own. Then he lifted his head, a tuft of dark hair falling forward over his brow.

'Friends!' he said bitterly.

Dazed, Peggy let him help her down and walk her towards the gate. The Rowans would object to strangers appearing in the driveway late at night and to members of their household staff keeping company at such late hours.

'Goodbye, Peggy!' called James, as she began to walk away from him.

'Good luck!' said Peggy, anxious to escape the temptation she had to fling her arms around him and beg him to kiss her once more. All she wanted was to get in that kitchen door, up the back stairs and into her room. For once she was glad that Kitty wasn't around, because all she wanted was peace and quiet and a chance to bawl her eyes out.

CHAPTER 11

The Big House

NOBODY COULD SAY FOR SURE HOW IT STARTED, but only a few days after the harvest home festival, the big house caught fire. Lord Henry and his family were all in their beds and the household staff fast asleep when, like a thief in the night, the first flame jumped through the broken window, catching the wooden frame and shutters. It chased its way across the heavy, century-old damask curtains, the dry fabric splitting and igniting. It raced downwards to the polished floorboards, then across the hand-crafted chairs and upwards over the pelmet to the beautiful plasterwork ceilings.

Finn, the great lumbering Irish wolfhound, Lord Henry's favourite of all his dogs, began to howl as he tried to escape from the huge, smoke-filled hallway. By now an inferno was raging in the elegant drawing-room and its curving bay window blew out onto the lawn.

Hearing some sort of commotion, Lord Henry roused himself, pulled on his silk dressing-gown and went to his bedroom window to see what was going on. But there was nobody outside. Suddenly he noticed the vivid orange flames reaching up over the bedroom windowsill and smoke seeping through the open cracks between the floorboards. Then a great roar came from the chimney at the side of the room, as if some enormous bellows were pumping air up it.

Lord Henry ran to the bed. 'Wake up, my dear! We must leave the house immediately.'

'What is it, Henry?' his wife asked crossly.

Passing her a dressing-gown he implored her to rouse herself as there was 'a bit of a fire'.

Lady Buckland began to scream for the children and servants, while her husband shoved the jewels on her dressing-table into his pocket. In an instant, the two girls stood in their nightgowns outside their bedroom doors. They stared, terrified, across the banister where they could see huge flames sweeping up the broad staircase.

'We must keep calm, my dears,' ordered Lord Henry. Finn jumped amongst them, barking madly, and growling down at the encroaching fire. At the same instant they all began to shout. 'WAKE UP! THERE'S A FIRE!'

The housekeeper appeared immediately, her hair wrapped in tight rags and clutching a leather valise. 'My valuables,' she stated firmly.

'Rouse the household!' yelled Lord Henry, praying that the butler heard him. 'We must go down the servants' stairs!' he said, leading the way through the small wooden door up on the half-landing. 'Make haste. These old houses are like tinderboxes.'

A smell of smoke permeated the small, enclosed space as they all hurried down the stairs, the large dog shoving ahead of them all and barking madly at the encroaching fire. The line increased rapidly as the rest of the staff filed down behind them. Half-afraid, Lord Henry shoved the door at the bottom of the staircase open, and stepped out into the tiled passageway, conscious of the loud cracking roar close by.

'Hurry up! Do hurry up!' he ordered curtly, and they all rushed out into the large kitchen. Bernard Delaney, the butler, now back in his own territory, busied himself unlocking the heavy door, trying to look in command of things, despite the fact that he was wearing only a pair of knee-britches.

'Hurry up, man!' ordered Lord Henry.

'Are all the servants up?' asked Lady Martha anxiously, regaining some of her composure.

'Where's Lizzie?' wondered Mary Keating, Lady Martha's personal maid, 'and that new girl?'

Mercy Farrell, who stood beside Mary, gasped. Lizzie Collins and the new girl, Dolores, slept right up at the very top of the house. Lizzie would sleep through anything after her long day's work and had been banished to the furthest room because of her loud snoring, and Dolores, who spent her whole time scouring out pots and pans and washing in the scullery, was half-simple, and mightn't know what was going on.

'They mustn't have heard us!' Mercy wailed.

The whole group stood silent as the plight of the young girls in the upstairs attic dawned on them.

'I'll run up and get them!' volunteered Mercy, 'they're my friends.'

'Are you sure, my dear?' asked Lady Martha, not certain it was wise to risk the life of another of her servant girls.

'I'm well used to racing up and down these stairs, your ladyship.' Turning on her heel, her dark hair streaming behind her, Mercy raced across the kitchen and back through the door and up the stairs while the others stumbled outside to safety.

Through the night air they could hear the farm bell ringing, calling the tenants to help.

Lord Henry led them around to the front of the house, where the true enormity of the fire struck them when they saw the roaring flames blaze through the windows and cover the whole front of the house.

'Oh my dear God!' cried Lady Martha, slumping on the lawn.

'We've got to try and save the house!' shouted Lord Henry. 'Fill buckets, pails, whatever receptacles you can find.' Total chaos and commotion followed as the frantic search for buckets began.

Finn raced around, half-crazy with excitement. 'For heaven's sake, Rose, get a piece of rope and tie up that dog!' yelled Lord Henry.

Within minutes the stableyard staff had arrived on the scene. Michael ran as fast as he could, heart pounding, alongside Toss and Tom and Liam and Paddy and young Brendan.

'Oh Michael! Toss! Bring buckets! The house is on fire!' Miss Felicia came running towards them in bare feet, wearing only her white cotton nightgown, her hair loose and wild.

Brendan and Paddy turned back down the avenue to go and get buckets. The others stopped in shock for an instant when they saw the blazing house, then they rushed to join the line of household staff and Lord Henry and Miss Rose, who had all formed a human chain. The chain extended from the side wing of the house across the gravelled walkway, along the herbaceous border and up the stone steps. Buckets were filled from the outside tap, then passed along the line as fast as everybody could manage it.

Soon the massive hall door had blistered and burnt and cracked, enabling them to kick it down. Someone poured water into the hallway, splashing it onto the sizzling flames and causing them to hiss momentarily. Toss and Bernard doused the old grandfather clock that stood in the hall, then, rushing across the floor, heaved it up and dragged it out the door, where everyone helped lift it awkwardly down the granite steps onto the lawn. The wood was still warm and one side rather blistered, but at least it was out of the house.

'Two of the maids are still upstairs!' shouted Felicia, 'one of the others has gone to help them.'

With a tug of his heart Michael realised that Mercy was missing from the chain and knew he must find her.

'Where are they, Felicia?' he shouted at the bewildered young girl.

'They sleep right up in the attic, Michael. Mercy went to get them.'

'Which way?'

'She went up the servants' stairs ...'

Michael was already racing across the yard and through the kitchen. 'Mercy!' he called.

The stairs were pitch black and when he tried to take them at the double he almost fell. He could hear the creaking roar of the fire as he climbed up through the darkness. 'Mercy! Are ye all right?'

The smoke was so thick it nearly choked him, making him cough and wheeze. There was so much noise that he couldn't make out if the young women were hearing him or not.

He climbed up further, holding onto the narrow banisters. The door onto the first landing glowed a fiery red and would probably explode in a few minutes. The fire was right behind it on the other side. He quickened his pace.

'Mercy!' he screamed hoarsely.

He thought he heard something. 'Up here! We're up here!' It was Mercy.

One more landing, and the sound of the fire had changed. High up here it had a strange, rumbling sound, like thunder that would engulf you.

Michael opened the tiny door into the attic space. He gasped when he saw that part of the ceiling and roof had already collapsed. Claws of flames which belched from the chimney had set fire to the beams.

'Oh, thank God!' murmured Mercy.

The other two girls were sitting mesmerised and terrified on the narrow bed. Mercy was trying to drag them away, but she couldn't get them to move.

'Out of here!' shouted Michael firmly, grabbing Dolores by the arm. 'Move!'

As if he had waved a magic wand, the two girls got to their feet. He had broken the spell.

He pulled up a bit of old, worn carpet off the ground. Follow me!' he ordered, trying to hide the quiver in his voice.

Mercy was holding a wound-up sheet. 'I damped this, Michael,' she said. Doubling the sheet around her neck she ran with the rest of them across the narrow landing, burning her hands as she touched the door leading to the stairway. It was slow going in the darkness, trying to manoeuvre down the winding, narrow wooden steps. It would be far easier to fall going downwards.

'Nobody talk!' said Michael. 'The air is too smoky.'

Mercy covered her mouth with the sheet and Lizzie, following behind, used the other end of it. The heat was getting more intense, the smoke choking them. They scrambled down as fast as they could. Suddenly the darkness disappeared and giant yellow-orange flames blazed up at them, blocking their path. They all stopped in a line. They were stuck. The door on the first landing had burst through and Michael could see that this whole section of the stairs had caught fire! He peered through the smoke. It seemed that only a section of the stairs was burning yet – if they could get through that bit, they should be safe.

'We must go through it!' Michael said quietly. The flames were racing upwards, second by second. The banisters were too hot to touch.

Quickly Mercy unwound the heavy sheet. 'It'll only give us a second or two,' she murmured.

She tossed it down in front of them, and as the flames died for that second or two, the four of them stumbled forward, ignoring the pain in their legs and feet. In a flash the fire had destroyed the water-soaked sheet, but they had all managed to jump away from it and tumble down the rest of the wooden steps.

Gasping and choking, they emerged out into the kitchen. Michael grabbed Mercy's hand as the four of them stumbled through the smoke and escaped out the door.

Dolores flung herself on the ground in shock; part of her frizzy hair was singed and her foot was blistered. She was confused and scared, and wailed quietly to herself.

'All I want is to throw meself in that lake and cool

down,' said Lizzie. 'I thought me hour had surely come!'

Michael took in the scene on the front lawn. More help had arrived. In the distance he could see Lord Henry directing operations. They had broken the large bay windows of his study on the side of the house overlooking the lake, and the men were lifting out books and tables and trying to drag out the massive mahogany desk which seemed to be stuck.

Michael let go of Mercy's hand. 'I'd better go and help, love. You stay here. I'll come back to you later, I promise, Mercy!'

He ran over to help with the lifting, ignoring the searing of pain he felt as he moved. The study was soaked. They were flinging bucket after bucket of water against the door, giving Paddy and Toss a chance to lift things out.

Young Brendan was way back down the line and Michael realised that he was calling him over.

'What is it, Brendan?' quizzed Michael, going to him.

'I'm right worried about the horses, Michael,' said Brendan.

'They'll be fine,' murmured Michael. 'They're far enough from the house.'

'I think we should go and check on them.' Before Michael could object, young Brendan took off, and, without knowing why, Michael followed after him down the avenue.

The smell of smoke was heavy in the air and the horses in the far paddock whinnied anxiously. The carriage-horses were going wild, nostrils flaring, as they kicked against the fencing, trying to escape the choking smoke that blew across from the yard.

As they rounded the final bend in the avenue they saw that the smaller haybarn was ablaze, and Michael knew instinctively from the silence of the two stables close beside it that the horses inside were already dead. Frantically, Brendan began to open the stable doors and lead the other horses out.

'Be careful!' Michael shouted. He knew how dazed and scared the animals would be, and watched transfixed as the terrified horses thrashed and kicked out when their door was opened. Troy's front legs and hooves caught the stable boy unawares. Brendan lay sprawled against the wall, blood gushing from his arm as Troy galloped way.

Michael cursed to himself under his breath. Why hadn't they left all of the horses outside? Why had they stabled any of them? He began to call to the horses, trying to make his voice sound normal, the way it was every morning when he came to see them, hoping they would recognise him.

Pippin, Miss Felicia's horse, whinnied. 'Good girl!' he told her gently. She was trembling with fear, her small fawn-coloured body quivering. He patted and stroked her neck, grabbing hold of her mane as he eased the door open, ready to push it shut if she started to rear. But Pippin was content to let him guide her across the yard to the company of the other horses in the paddock. The low, timber frame of her stall crackled and burst into flames behind her, hay and straw lighting up in seconds.

Michael decided to throw open all the doors and let the horses run free, and hope they wouldn't panic and injure themselves. He ran from one door to another, pulling back the heavy iron bolts and flinging open the doors.

Glengarry was covered in sweat and thrashing at her door, trying to get out. In a far corner, Morning Boy rolled his eyes in terror. The mare had given herself a few knocks, and, confused with pain and fear, was making the situation worse for both herself and her foster foal. Michael realised that if she got out she would just gallop till she dropped or batter herself against anything that got in her way. But what would happen to the foal then?

'Get me a halter, and the canvas one for the foal,' Michael shouted, hoping that Brendan had recovered enough to help him. Seconds later the boy was back with them. Slipping off his shirt, Michael climbed over the door, balancing on top of it as he tried to avoid Glengarry's hooves. With the halter over his shoulder, Michael reached up for the mare's head, surprising her when he flung his shirt over her nose and across her eyes, blocking out the sight of the pandemonium around her. A second later Michael had slipped the halter on her.

'Open the door, Brendan,' he yelled.

He held firmly onto the mare, who reared up and tried to kick away from him. Michael struggled to hold her as she bucked, but once he got her outside the stable she allowed him to lead her across the yard. Brendan ran over and opened the paddock gate to let her in, then closed it behind them. Glengarry was safe.

The two boys ran back to the stable for the foal. Michael slipped the familiar canvas halter over the foal's head and began to pull the terrified young horse outside. The colt jerked backwards, careering into the red-hot door. He started to jump and kick as he felt the burning wood scorch his side, singeing his skin, and Michael and Brendan barely managed to hold him. But out in the yard they finally calmed him down and were able to coax him into the paddock and reunite him with Glengarry.

By the time Toss came to the burnt-out stables searching for them, Michael and Brendan had saved most of the horses – many of them had simply disappeared, galloped off to God knows where, and would have to be rounded up tomorrow. The two lads had doused the flames in the harness room and prevented it from being destroyed. But the haybarn was gone, and the carriage-house all but ruined.

'Good God!' shouted Toss, his eyes raking across the scene of destruction. 'There's no way the flames could have spread here from the house. This fire is a deliberate act, carried out by some blackguard,' he said, narrowing his eyes.

Michael and Brendan nodded miserably, the boss voicing their own inner thoughts. The burning of Castletaggart House and stables was definitely no accident. And Michael had his suspicions.

*   *   *

Michael watched as the house continued to burn. This was the beginning of the end of a way of life. The air was heavy with the smell of burning timber and plaster, a choking, thick, all-enveloping sensation that filled your nostrils and mouth till it lay heavy in the very pit of your stomach.

Castletaggart House glowed livid red, its gaping,

empty windows touched with a raging blaze of colour. Flames danced and jeered through the roof, bursting from all the tall chimneys. No buckets of water, no fire-wagon, no chain of human fire-fighters could stop it now as the fire completed its joyful victory.

The large hall where kind old Lady Buckland had been waked, where the Castletaggart hunt had met, where visitors had called to pay their respects, was now a huge, open, gaping, pain-filled mouth as the old house lay dying.

Those who had helped gave up only when Lord Henry called a halt. Defeated, he walked slowly down the line of helpers. 'It's no use, my friends! We can do no more!' His broad face was reddened from the heat, and there were dark shadows of exhaustion under his eyes.

The maids and cook and many of the other staff began to sob as the buckets were dropped and the pump stilled. A hush fell over them all while the fire raged on, consuming everything in front of it.

In total silence, Rose Buckland and her mother stood like two ghosts, watching their home being destroyed.

*　*　*

Noticing a flurry of noise, Michael became aware of the arrival of yet more tenants. They held themselves apart under some huge chestnut trees, watching. Michael couldn't see them clearly, but he thought he could make out Peadar amongst them.

Then a carriage and two horses turned up along the avenue and Michael recognised Philip Delahunt, a friend of the master's. Grim-faced, Mr Delahunt drew up in front of the house. Michael ran forward, offering to hold the horses.

'Good God! How on earth did this happen?' Mr Delahunt asked, stepping down. 'Where are Henry and the family?' Michael pointed out the family to him.

Philip Delahunt had a gruff manner and was not one for idle chit-chat. He stood for about five minutes watching the house, then strode down to join Lady Buckland and Rose on the lawn. He was obviously arguing with them. Soon Lord Henry joined in the conversation, the result of which was that the ladies walked slowly to the carriage with Mr Delahunt.

Suddenly, a lone voice called from under the chestnut trees: 'Burn them out!'

Lady Buckland raised her head and tightened the belt of her dressing-gown around her. She tilted her chin proudly, and through barely open lips muttered, 'Rose! Don't say one word!'

Rose swallowed hard and her eyes filled with tears, but she obeyed, following her mother into the carriage.

'Where is Felicia?' asked Lady Buckland, her voice quivering.

'She's over there,' said Michael, pointing to the young girl, who was marching in her nightclothes towards the chestnut trees, her auburn hair loose. Michael chased through the crowds after her.

Felicia stopped in front of the group under the trees. Standing there wild-eyed, in her white flowing cotton nightgown with her pale skin and wild hair, she looked for all the world like a banshee.

'I heard what you said!' she screamed. 'I know what you did!'

Michael grabbed her by the elbow. 'Come on, Miss Felicia, you'll catch your death. Your mother and Miss Rose and Mister Delahunt are all waiting for you.'

'I hate you!' she yelled, ignoring him. 'Each and every one of you! Keep your stinking dirty cabins. You've destroyed the finest house in the county. My father is a good man – he's done his best for all of you, and this is how you pay him back!'

'Please, Miss!' begged Michael, tugging at her. The eleven-year-old girl looked fit to collapse.

'Go back to England!' someone muttered.

Felicia stopped for a second as if she had been shot. 'I was born in that front room there.' She pointed towards the house. 'I am as Irish as any of the rest of you. But you don't care about that. If we go away who will you blame then? I'll tell you what'll happen.' She laughed hysterically. 'You'll all fight among yourselves, that's what my father says. You'll fight and kill each other one by one, that's what you'll do. Each and every one of you can go to hell. See if we care!'

The crowd was silent as she turned away from them.

'I'm cold, Michael.' She shivered.

Michael didn't know what to think as he helped the angry young girl up to the waiting arms of her mother and sister.

'I'm so sorry for all that's happened,' he said, taking a deep breath. But the three women seemed not to hear him. The carriage turned, the wheels skidding on the gravel, and they drove off down the avenue and away from Castletaggart House.

CHAPTER 12

Partings and Promises

CASTLETAGGART HOUSE BURNED FOR HOURS, the huge beams still smouldering when daylight came. Finn lay across the bottom step in front of the door, guarding the house despite the heat and sounds that rumbled from inside.

Someone had arrived with clothes for Lord Henry, and he marched around the outside of the building engrossed in serious conversation with Philip Delahunt, his manager George Darker, and two more of his acquaintances. Toss had told him about the stables, but Lord Henry seemed unable to take in the news.

The furniture and books and possessions that had survived had been lifted onto carts and taken off to be put in storage.

The parlour maids, the cook, the kitchen staff, the

tutor, Bernard the butler – all sat on the grass, exhausted. Michael hunkered down too, and leant against a beech tree, stretching out his legs and listening to the wind rustle through the leaves. He was so tired he felt that if he closed his eyes he would sleep forever. He thought of Morning Boy and his mother Ragusa, and of all the horses he'd cared for here, of all the good times he'd had since he first came to work in the big house, and how proud he'd been of his first proper job and the chance to work with such magnificent horses. Every day he'd ridden past this house admiring its beauty, its solid strength, wondering what the rooms were like inside. It was a world apart. At times perhaps he did envy it, but always there had been a respect.

The old house groaned as the whole back section came crumbling to the ground. Tears filled Michael's eyes as he thought of all the good times a house like that must have had.

'What are you snivelling about?' Toss stood in front of him, legs apart.

Michael wiped his nose on the sleeve on his smoke-soaked vest, swallowing hard. 'The house, Toss. Honest to God, I'll miss the house – seeing it, ye know,' he replied.

With a strange ferocity, Toss almost punched him. 'You want to cry, Michael O'Driscoll? Then cry over this, the land. This land can feed our horses, feed our cows, give us a rich crop to harvest. What do ye think will happen the land now when the landlords go? It'll be townies and middle-men that will decide and fight over it. Half the people you see around you will be off their land in a week or two. Irish men will fight Irish men. Just like the famine that spread amongst us, this fire – this fire, I'm telling you, will spread across the land. Things will never be the same.'

Michael was puzzled. What was Toss on about? He must have had a drop of whiskey or something. It was strange, but Miss Felicia had said something similar.

'There's work to be done, Michael!' Toss said sharply. 'The horses need us. You're to get back to work.'

Unprotesting, Michael got to his feet. Taking a last look at the smouldering shell of the big house, Michael walked back down towards the paddocks.

*   *   *

It was two days before Lord Henry appeared back on the estate, arriving in Mr Delahunt's trap.

Toss made the grooms and stable lads line up. No one had had much to eat or drink or a chance to sleep, so that they all looked rough and dishevelled. Lord Henry himself looked ten years older and seemed distant.

'My good men, I wish to thank you all for the Trojan efforts you made on Tuesday night, they are very much appreciated.' He coughed, his eyes glancing across the fenced paddocks and the burnt-out stables and coming to rest on Old Tom's stall. 'The overall loss has been huge – enormous – as you can imagine.'

'You can rebuild the house, your lordship, rebuild the stables,' murmured Pat, hope in his voice.

His words hung in the still air.

'I don't think so,' said Lord Henry slowly. 'My family and I propose to move to our house in London; there is also a small holding in Suffolk which my uncle left me a few years ago. I'm afraid Castletaggart House will not be rebuilt, at least not by me.'

'But what about our jobs? What about the horses?' shouted Liam Quigley.

'Well, that's what I was coming to, my good man. I'm afraid I will be unable to continue your employment. I will no longer need hunters or want to continue breeding racehorses here in Ireland.'

Michael's head was reeling. Now he had no job, no place to stay.

'My family and I would like to thank you all for your many loyal years of service,' continued the landlord. 'My good friend Philip Delahunt has agreed to buy a few ponies and some of the workhorses – he has no interest in racing, unfortunately. The rest of the stock will be sold off or disposed of in due course. Toss, may I have a word with you?'

Lord Henry took Toss aside for a few minutes while they all stood in silence, waiting. At last Lord Henry returned to address them again.

'I wish each and every one of you good luck in finding new positions,' he said formally. 'Mr Byrne here will provide you with good references. I believe that there are wages due to some of you. No doubt you will realise I am hardly flush with cash at the present time, but I do promise to try and recompense you for your loyalty and work as soon as I am able.'

Shaking Toss's hand, the landlord turned around to return to the trap.

Michael's head was full of questions, about his job, his work, his future, but his deepest concern at the moment was for Morning Boy and Glengarry, both recovering in the last paddock. Forgetting himself, Michael chased after Lord Henry.

'Excuse me, sir! What about the mare Glengarry and Morning Boy?'

Lord Henry stopped.

Michael jumped in front of him. 'They're over here, sir!' he said, leading the way. Lord Henry and Toss followed.

The mare was nervous, standing with one foot lifted slightly.

'She's lame, Lord Henry,' said Toss. 'She kicked against the stall.'

Morning Boy stood close to her, ears flat, ignoring them. His head was turned as he tried to lick at the blistered side of his back, while he smelt the ointment that Toss had helped Michael rub on him.

Lord Henry squinted in the sunlight, looking at them both.

'He's Ragusa's foal,' Michael interrupted his thoughts, knowing that the colt looked anything but a champion at the moment.

'Of course! Ragusa was one of the best fillies ever,' murmured Lord Henry. 'A great racehorse. Toss, do you think we could get the two of them to Suffolk with us next week?'

Toss looked at the mare and the frightened colt. ''Twould be too much for them. The mare's not a lot of good now. No, they wouldn't survive such a long journey.'

Michael tried to hide the sadness that choked him as the horses' fate was decided. Racehorses were temperamental and needed a lot of care and looking after. Being bred for speed, highly-strung and sensitive, they weren't much good for anything else.

No-one would buy them in this condition.

'How much money do I owe you, lad?' asked Lord Henry suddenly.

'Two months,' said Michael, looking down at the ground, embarrassed.

'Would you consider taking one of them in payment for money owed? I want you to know, too, that I'm very grateful for the heroism you displayed in rescuing some of the female staff on Tuesday.'

Michael nodded, not sure if he was being given the colt or the sad-eyed mare.

'Begging your pardon, your Lordship,' interrupted Toss, 'them two are a pair and Michael here would be the only one with a chance of making something of either of them. Let him have the two.'

Michael stood stock still, trying to disguise the warm feeling of hope coursing through his veins.

'Deserves a chance then, does he? Well, I suppose I should give them both to him, part payment and part reward. They're yours, young man, all yours.'

'Thank you, sir, I'll do my level best with the horses. They'll be looked after, that I promise you.'

'I'll take your word, then, Michael O'Driscoll, I'll take your word for it.' Lord Henry Buckland returned to the trap, clicking the horse on to take him away from the stableyard, the place he had loved.

*   *   *

Michael let what had happened sink in. Imagine, he was the new owner of Glengarry and Morning Boy!

'You stupid eejit,' shouted Pat Gallagher. 'What use are the like of those horses to you? You should have waited for your proper wages. The mare is too lame, you know she should be put down by rights. How the heck are you going to feed the likes of those two when the winter sets in, or keep them warm and dry?'

'Michael, are you mad!' argued Brian. 'You could have gone to England or America. What's the use of being lumbered with two horses that aren't much good?'

Michael shrugged. Perhaps his friends were right. How could the likes of him keep such horses?

Toss didn't say much. 'I'm moving to England with the family to see what's what over there. I'll try out the place for a while, anyway, since there's not much on offer for me here.'

By late afternoon a procession of servants started to file down the long avenue, carrying whatever bits and pieces they'd managed to save from the fire. Michael waited till he spotted Mercy Farrell's toss of dark hair. They ran and embraced each other.

'Mercy! Where are you going?' he asked.

'I'm going back home, Michael. My folks will be right surprised to see me after such a long time, let me tell you. Lizzie is going to England with the family but they don't have need of any more household staff.' Mercy looked at him anxiously. 'And you, Michael? What are you going to do?'

'Oh Mercy! I wish none of this had happened. Now I've nothing to offer you.' He held her hand, feeling miserable and lonely.

'It'll be all right, Michael. I'm only going to Athlone, my old home town. Ask anybody where Paddy Farrell's is and they'll point ye to my father's blacksmith's yard. I won't be too far away.'

He tilted her face to his, kissing her eyelids and nose, and lastly her soft, warm lips.

'I won't forget you, Michael, my love,' she breathed gently.

'I'll find you, Mercy. When everything is right, I promise.'

Michael cursed the blackguards responsible for all this – Peadar and his cohorts. They had ruined everything around them. Now even the girl he loved was going from him too. She kissed him one last time before getting on her way, leaving him on the tree-lined avenue behind her.

*　*　*

Michael remembered that when he was a youngster, just a little lad, he would bring every injured animal or bird that he found home to the shop in Castletaggart, and there in the back kitchen his two great-aunts, Nano and Lena, and his sister, Eily, would fuss over the poor creature and help him take care of it. The shop was long gone, but maybe he could go to his older sister and her family? Eily was good and kind and sensible. She'd know what to do. John and herself would help with the horses, he was sure of it. They had a farm, just a small holding, but at least it would be somewhere safe for himself and the horses for a while. Yes, that's what he would do. Once the horses had healed up a bit and were ready for the road, that was the very place Michael would go. It would be just wonderful to see Eily and Nano and Mary-Brigid and little Jodie and John once more.

CHAPTER 13

Night Watch

EILY PACED UP AND DOWN the flag-stone floor as darkness wrapped itself around the cottage and filled the small window panes.

'What ails ye, child?' enquired Nano anxiously. 'You've wiped that table top at least three times and you're making Mary-Brigid and myself dizzy with your to-ing and fro-ing. You're like a hen on a hot griddle! For heaven's sake, will ye sit down and relax for a while!'

'I'm really worried, Nano,' Eily sighed, running her fingers through her hair. 'John should have been home at least two hours ago and still there's no sign of him! Do you think something might have happened to him?'

'Shush, Eily!' cautioned Nano, touching her finger to her lips as she noticed Mary-Brigid lift her head and look over from the mat near the fire, where she was playing with Scrap, the orange kitten. 'He'll be along soon, I'm sure, Eily. You'll see, he'll have a good reason for missing his meal.'

'Aye, maybe you're right,' murmured Eily, trying to calm herself as she peered out into the blackness yet again. 'Mary-Brigid, you should have been in bed hours ago. You'll be falling asleep in school tomorrow. Come on, I'll tuck you in.'

Mary-Brigid gave a huge yawn. She didn't want to go to bed when her daddy wasn't home. What if he'd got lost in the woods or the fairies had taken him? 'No!' she said stubbornly. 'I must stay awake till Daddy comes.'

Her mother knelt down near her. 'Listen, pet, I know you're worried and scared, just the same as I am, but you have to sleep. I promise that just as soon as Daddy comes in he'll go and say goodnight to you.'

Mary-Brigid still tickled the kitten's pale tummy fur, considering. 'Can Scrap sleep at the bottom of the bed tonight, then?'

'Why, you little weasel!' teased her mother. 'Poor Nano mightn't fancy sharing the bed with the cat!'

'Please, Nano!' begged Mary-Brigid. 'Please! Please!'

'Why is it that the child can always wheedle her way around me?' said Nano, leaving down the sock she was darning. 'You can take the cat for a while for company, but he'll have to make do with the kitchen when I decide to go to bed.'

'Thank you, Nano! You're the best auntie in the world,' smiled Mary-Brigid sleepily, clutching the kitten as she followed her mother.

Two more hours had passed and Nano had dozed off – she had insisted on waiting up with Eily. Suddenly from outside, Eily heard two strange male voices. Scared, she reached for the long iron poker resting on the hearth. They were coming nearer the house. What did they want? Maybe they were drunk or something? Then they tapped lightly on the door.

'Missus, open up!' someone called. 'Don't be afraid – we won't harm you.'

'Go away!' she whispered loudly.

'Missus! We've your man, John, with us. Open up and let us in!'

Eily stood stock still, not knowing whether to believe him or not.

'Eily! Eily!' She recognised her husband's voice immediately, and she rushed to open the door. John was there, being supported by two strangers; he was barely able to stand.

'God almighty!' Eily screamed.

'There was a bit of a fight, Mrs Powers, at the tenants' meeting and –'

'What? Who were you fighting? John, how did you get involved in this? Are you hurt bad?' Eily screamed in confusion at her young husband.

The men ignored her and lowered John down onto the old fireside chair.

'Ahhh!' he moaned in pain.

'He'll be fine, missus. It just looks a lot worse than it is,' mumbled the older, grey-haired man, as he shuffled, half-embarrassed, to the door.

'Thank you very much for bringing him home,' Eily said woodenly, longing for these strangers and the trouble they'd brought to be out of her home. As if reading her mind, they slipped away back into the night. With relief, she closed the door behind them. 'John, what in heaven's name happened?'

'I was at a tenants' meeting,' he muttered through swollen, bleeding lips. 'But it was afterwards it happened, when we started to walk home. Paddy Hennessy ran into that gombeen man, Hussey, the agent. He started shouting at him and calling him names. Hussey told him to stop, but you know what Paddy's like when he's riled. He must have gone crazy because he went for Hussey, jumping right on him, swinging out of his jacket. Then Hussey took a swipe at him and Hennessy went mad altogether. Next thing I knew, the two of them were on the ground kicking and punching the daylights out of each other. Myself and a few of the lads tried to break it up, and then Hussey's friends came out of the hotel and decided to have a go at us. We had to try and defend ourselves, Eily.'

John's face was badly bruised and cut, one eye totally swollen and closed. Both his hands were bloodied, knuckles torn and sore. Under his shirt, his skin was almost pulped where the mark of heavy hob-nailed boots had been stamped across his ribcage.

Eily filled a basin with warm water, and began to bathe and clean his wounds with a towel.

Nano stirred. Her eyes opened wide when she saw the state John was in. She came over to comfort him.

'I'm all right, Nano,' he grimaced, trying to make light of it. 'I just got caught in the middle of a fight.'

The old lady fussed over him and insisted on making him a cup of tea. He did his best to drink it, though it burned his cracked, sore lips. Once his face was cleaned, and all the blood washed away, the swelling and bruising could be seen clearly.

'What a mess!' he tried to joke, as they both looked at him.

'Who did this to you, my love?' Eily asked, stroking his cheek gently.

'A few right boyos, friends of Hussey's. But I think it was a constable that got my nose!'

'A constable! Oh my God, John, what will happen now?' Eily moaned.

'I don't know,' he sighed wearily, hiding his face in his hands.

'You don't know!' screamed Eily, almost hysterical. 'We might have a constable banging on our door in the morning, and all you can say is you don't know!'

'Hush, Eily!' soothed Nano. 'Did anyone recognise you, John?'

'Well, maybe Hussey did. But, Nano, I swear I didn't lay a finger on him. Paddy beat him up real bad ... I didn't know any of the others as far as I can remember.'

'Are you sure, John?' questioned Nano, gazing seriously at him.

'Aye, Nano! I'm fair sure and certain.'

'Then we just have to pray that trouble stays away from this door,' she murmured. 'That's all we can do. The police will be after Paddy. They'll hunt him down.'

Eily sat down opposite John, her eyes almost closed as she tried to hide the mounting sense of fear within her and her anger at John's putting their tenancy at risk.

'I think I'll away to my bed,' said Nano diplomatically, and she disappeared into the small back room she shared with Mary-Brigid.

Eily listened as John told her about the new landlord Dennis Ormonde's plans to merge many of the small holdings and farms, getting rid of what he considered the poor and useless tenants – like old Agnes. Hussey himself was supposed to be getting one of these newer, enlarged farms, so naturally it was in his best interests to rid Ormonde's land of as many small tenants as possible. The landlord was keen to sell – there were rumours of large betting debts. Without a doubt he was going to put up the rents, which would drive more people away.

'Put the rent up! Again? John, how can we possibly manage that?' sobbed Eily.

'No-one is going to put me off the land that my family have farmed for generations,' John said firmly. 'Eily, this land should rightfully be ours and I'll not give it up without a fight.'

'Would he sell this holding?' she whispered.

'Maybe,' John shrugged his shoulders. 'But some are saying that us tenants should have the first right to buy at a fair price!'

'Sure, what use would that be if we don't have the money? They have us caught!' said Eily angrily. 'You know we could never afford to buy our farm.'

John stared moodily at the dying embers of the fire. 'This is our home, Eily, and we've both worked hard on this land. They might evict a poor old woman like Agnes because she can no longer grow crops or fix up her cabin, but they'll not evict us. I've no intention of letting them take our land!'

'Promise?' she said softly.

'I promise,' said John hoarsely, reaching for her hand.

CHAPTER 14

The Secret

MARY-BRIGID GASPED when she saw her father's face next morning. She watched, perplexed, as he walked slowly around the kitchen as if all his bones hurt. His left eye had turned a horrible purple-black colour.

'Daddy! Daddy! What happened to you?' she screamed, half-afraid.

'I was in a bit of a fight, pet, and now I'll have to take it easy for a few days.'

Mary-Brigid's head was full of questions about who her father had been fighting and why, but one look at her mother's white face and blotchy, tear-stained eyes, told her not to say too much.

'Hurry along, Mary-Brigid, or you'll be late for school!' urged Eily, lacing up the child's heavy black brogues and fetching a small can of milk and a wrapped chunk of soda bread for her.

Mary-Brigid ran to say goodbye to her father before
setting off on the three-quarters-of-a-mile walk with her
mother to the small white-washed school at the cross-
roads.

'Ouch!' he said, as she flung her arms around his
neck. 'Listen, pet, not a word about this to your teacher
or any of your friends, d'ye hear?'

'Yes, Daddy.'

'If anyone asks you, Mary-Brigid, your daddy was at
home here with us all night,' added Eily.

Mary-Brigid stared from one to the other. She didn't
understand a bit of it, and now her mammy and daddy
wanted her to tell a lie on top of everything else.

''Twill be a lie,' she said softly.

''Twill be a fib,' said her mother, 'and one that you
will tell if anyone asks you. You're a big girl now and
you know enough not to discuss the goings-on of last
night with anyone.'

'Aye,' agreed Mary-Brigid, who, if the truth be told,
felt more like a small scared girleen than a big girl who
could be trusted to keep a secret.

The Hennessys were gone. Not a single one of the
boys came to school and the schoolmaster was right
annoyed with them. Joe Clancy, a twelve-year-old
neighbour, had called to the cottage door, only to find

it wide open. There wasn't a trace of the twins or any of the family. They'd all scarpered.

'Gone! Just gone!' he told the whole class, as Mary-Brigid pretended to look at the map of Ireland on the wall and tried to make sense of what was going on.

The next few days she spent helping Eily with the heavy chores, trying to hold the cow steady as her mother milked it, and helping to clean out the small, stinking pigpen, while her father remained hidden indoors until the bruises on his face began to fade.

She missed the twins. 'Twas lucky that she had the little cat to remember them by. She couldn't help but wonder where they had run off to. At school Sally Nolan told her that the police were searching for Mr Hennessy. They said that he had half-killed the land agent and if they caught him he'd be put in prison forever or hung.

Mary-Brigid could hardly play or sleep with the worry of it all, and her dreams were haunted by the vision of her daddy in irons and chains being transported to some far-off land.

CHAPTER 15

The Gift

 MICHAEL PATTED MORNING BOY'S SILKY COAT. The large burn on his side had started to heal, the skin and hair finally knitting together. Glengarry was busy grazing, her long neck bent, her jaws chomping on the blades of grass. One hoof was held at an awkward angle, not supporting her properly. Both horses were still recovering from the fire. All the other horses had gone at this stage, sold off to the highest bidders, a few going to England.

Young Brendan had been offered a job with Mr Delahunt. 'I'll still see some of our horses, Michael,' he said. 'Won't that be grand?'

Michael had to suppress a pang of jealousy as he saw the younger lad's eager and excited face.

Toss Byrne had come down to the stables as the horses were being sold off, moving among the burnt-out buildings. He gave Michael a horse-blanket, two worn bridles and two full sets of harness. Toss said goodbye to the horses in his own fashion. Michael watched the way he went up to each one of them, right up close, his head and lips almost touching their pointed ears, talking to them, whispering to them.

Michael watched as the old man walked towards Glengarry, his voice slow and soothing, getting her to lift her head and listen to him.

'Michael!' He beckoned, and Michael swung himself up over the wooden fence into the paddock.

Toss was whispering away in a low voice to the horse.

'Michael, stand beside me! Listen to me!' ordered Toss. Michael came nearer. 'Michael, you already have the gift of handling horses,' said Toss. 'You like them and care about them and they know and feel it. They trust you because you treat them like intelligent animals, recognising that they get sad and nervous, and angry and scared, and happy and giddy, just like we humans do.'

'Aye!' agreed Michael.

'Michael, you know I have no children, no sons. Today I want to give you a gift – well, much of it you already have. This was passed from my father to me. He got it from his father before him. Move right up close by me.' Michael stood beside the horse, his hand stroking her side. 'Just listen!'

Toss began to whisper and Michael could make out the horse's name, Glengarry. Toss whispered of wind in the trees and green grass growing, of soft rain that fell, and night sky that drew in and stars that watched from above. He spoke of horses that pulled and ploughed and helped man to till the earth that God gave them. He told of horses that carried men into battle in the names of kings and queens, of all the animal kingdom large and small, and of the horse's place as a friend of man.

Glengarry stood totally still, listening, ears pricked, eyes wide and alert as the whispering went on. Toss spoke of times past, times present and times to come. He spoke of the races she'd run, the foals she'd had and would have, and the races they too would run.

Michael barely dared to breathe. Toss whispered to Glengarry of the life-blood that coursed through her body, the energy that must travel to heal her damaged leg and hoof. She seemed to whinny softly, blowing air down her velvety nostrils. Her heart seemed to beat strong and steady as the voice talked on and on to her.

As Michael listened the words changed. They did not

seem like normal words, but ran together – it wasn't
Gaelic or English or French. But he could sort of
understand it, just the way Glengarry seemed to.

Then Toss's voice trailed off. Glengarry sniffed at the
man's head and hair, and Toss patted her playfully.

'Aye! She's a good one, Michael, a right good one,'
said the older man as they walked back across the field.

'Thank you, Toss!' said Michael. 'I've never heard the
gift of whispering before, it's a rare thing.'

'Now you must try it. It'll help you with the horses
in future, Michael, mark my words. Call Morning Boy!'

The young horse loved attention and cantered over
immediately. Michael was nervous as he bent towards
Morning Boy's neck. 'Morning Boy, born as the moon
dipped and the sun rose warm from earth ...' whispered
Michael.

*   *   *

It was only a few days' walk to Eily's home. Michael
took it good and easy with the horses. Glengarry's leg
was improving, but she was still fairly lame.

Walking through the open countryside reminded Michael of the time before when, hungry and scared,
dressed in rags and starving, he had walked – walked
because his very life had depended on it – with his sisters,
Eily and Peggy, at the height of the Great Famine.

He gave a sigh of relief when he finally reached the townland where Eily's cottage was. He had so much to tell them all, about the fire, and the Bucklands, and his two horses. Another mile or two and he would see the whitewash of his sister's cottage, where old aunt Nano would make him sit down like a travelling storyteller and go through all that had happened. He grinned to himself, longing to see them all again.

CHAPTER 16

The Visitor

TO TELL THE TRUTH, Mary-Brigid was glad to be outside
and away from the cottage. Ever since the night her
father had come home all bruised and cut, it was if a
dark shadow, like a big black crow, had spread its
wings and settled itself over them all.

She didn't rightly understand it, and no-one had
explained it to her, but it had something to do with the
landlord and what had happened to old Agnes and the
sudden disappearance of the Hennessys.

Her mother and father had changed too. Nowadays
they were mostly quiet, as if they were watching and
waiting for something to happen. Auntie Nano prayed
and prayed – Mary-Brigid had never seen anyone pray
so much. The old lady's lips moved even in her sleep,

and Mary-Brigid could almost hear the words of a prayer. Jodie, even though he was only a small boy, sensed that all was not well and had become cranky and cross, and had her tormented with wanting to play and be distracted.

At least outside, with the soft breeze blowing and the white clouds scudding across the sky, they could try and forget about it.

'Jodie!' she shouted. 'Look at the heron!'

Her brother's dark, curly head turned skywards and they both watched the huge bird spread its wings and lift its long legs as it flapped to gain more height, flying slowly in a wide circle over their farm.

'What's he looking for?' asked Jody.

'A fish. A little flap from a fish in the stream or in the lake,' she said, wondering if the heron could see them at all.

As the bird flew out of sight, Mary-Brigid became aware of the gentle clip-clop of a horse close by. She listened, wondering who would be out so near their home at this hour of the day. She had strict instructions to run home as quick as lightning if she caught sight of the landlord or any of his men, or, God forbid, the constable!

She held her breath, waiting to grab Jodie and run with him. Then she spotted the familiar dark curly hair and kind open face of Michael, her mother's brother. He was leading two horses, a fine big strong-looking one, though she seemed to be walking lame, and the most beautiful foal that Mary-Brigid had ever seen.

'Michael!' she screamed. 'Uncle Michael!'

She ran like a whirlwind to met him, her dress flying around her as she raced across the tussocks of grass.

The two horses stopped, curious. Her uncle lifted her into his arms and hugged her.

'Why, Mary-Brigid, you're still the prettiest girl I know!' he said, ruffling her wild, fair hair.

She was so excited that she could hardly speak. Jodie had clambered down to stand beside her, watching them. 'This is Jodie!' she said, pushing him forward.

'I remember him,' grinned Michael, 'but he's got as big as a house! He's so strong I can barely lift him!'

Jodie chuckled as he was scooped up and hugged too. The little boy tugged at Michael's cap and his uncle gave it to him. 'Will ye mind that for me, Jodie?' he asked. Jodie nodded proudly. Nobody had ever let him mind anything before.

'How's everybody, Mary-Brigid? I'm dying to see them all.'

Mary-Brigid hesitated, only for a second or two, but Michael spotted it. His twinkling eyes became serious.

'Grand,' she mumbled softly, knowing he didn't

believe her. 'Mammy's a bit sad,' she explained, looking
down at the dust and stones and mud, 'she's worried
about things, all sorts of things that are going on.'

'Hmm,' Michael replied. 'Maybe it's just as well I
happened to come to see you all then!'

'Who owns the horses?' asked Mary-Brigid.

'I do, pet! They're both mine.'

'Yours!'

'Aye, I know, I can scarce believe it myself.'

'Who gave them to you? Did you buy them?' she
asked.

''Tis a long story, pet, and the rest of them will want
to hear it too. All I'll tell you at the moment is that the
mare is called Glengarry and the foal is Morning Boy.'

'Can I ride them, Uncle Michael? Will you teach me?'
she pleaded.

'They're not fit to be ridden at the moment, dotey,
but I promise to teach you once they're able for it.'

Mary-Brigid nearly jumped with joy. She'd been up
on a donkey, but never, ever on a proper horse.

'Me too!' copied Jodie, clasping and unclasping his
hands with all the excitement.

'You too. I promise,' said their uncle seriously.

Mary-Brigid knew that Michael was the kind of
person who kept promises and wouldn't let you down.
She was mighty glad he'd come to visit them. Maybe

all her great grand-aunt's prayers had been answered.

'Nano! Mammy! Daddy! Come quick!' she began to shout, running on up to the house ahead of him. 'Mammy, it's Michael. He's come to stay with us! He has horses!'

CHAPTER 17

The Homecoming

THERE HAD NEVER BEEN SUCH A HOMECOMING. Nano sat on her chair, blowing her nose loudly every now and then into a white handkerchief. Eily kept on hugging and embracing Michael.

'I'm right glad to see you, Michael. You'll never know how glad.'

John stood silent, and clasped Michael firmly by the hand in welcome. Michael sensed that something bad had happened, and, from the look of it, John had been in some sort of fight recently. He'd hear about it all in time.

A simple meal was prepared and they all gathered around the scrubbed, wooden table to eat. There was a huge bowl of potatoes, with freshly churned butter and a shake of salt. There was a cool jug of Bella's milk, and a plateful of spring onions which the adults sprinkled on their spuds. Eily blessed herself and said a special thanksgiving Grace for the food on the table and the return of her much-loved brother. 'Amen' echoed happily around the table.

Afterwards, Mary-Brigid helped Nano to clear the table and wash up. She knew that her mother and father and uncle had a lot to talk about, so once she was finished she slipped back outside to play and to have another look at the two horses her uncle had left grazing down in the low field.

Michael's homecoming seemed to bring a new energy and life to the small cottage. And more than that – he brought them hope.

'This is the finest holding in the district, John, no landlord in his right mind would get rid of such a good tenant, let alone such a good and useful farmhand!' he assured his brother-in-law.

John Powers nodded his head. Perhaps he was worrying needlessly. Michael knew more about the gentry and landlords than he would ever know. He'd be better off trying to put this fear out of his head and get on with his day-to-day work. Anyway, rumour had it that Dennis Ormonde had taken himself back to England for a few weeks, and, as his agent, William

Hussey, was still laid up after the bad beating he'd received, things would be peaceful enough for a while.

There was much to be done as the summer sun blazed across the land, and the fields and crops and animals all clamoured for attention. Michael was pleased to help. At night he would talk with Eily of the happy and sad days when they were young, growing up in their small cottage in Duneen, where the hawthorn tree grew and their baby sister lay buried. Those had been awful times during the Great Hunger, and the memory of them seemed to be almost part of the O'Driscoll family, a big bruise that would never fade away.

Then one morning, when they least expected it, a knock came on the door while they were having their porridge.

Mary-Brigid leaped from her stool and ran to answer it. ''Tis a stranger!' she whispered softly back to the rest of them.

Her father tucked his shirt into his trousers and came to the door. The man standing there had a small ginger moustache that jumped up and down as he talked. He spoke to John in a low voice and Mary-Brigid did her best to eavesdrop and catch what they were saying.

'Due to certain circumstances and considerations, Mr Ormonde has no other option but to increase the rent.'

'Increase the rent!' shouted her father. 'What happens if I don't pay this increase – won't pay it?'

'Then, unfortunately, Mr Powers, you would be served a notice to quit.'

John thumped his fist against the door frame. ''Tis not fair!' he protested.

'I'm afraid fairness doesn't come into it. This is business. Please understand I am acting on behalf of your landlord and under the instructions of Mr Hussey.'

'Hussey!' shouted John. 'I knew that rat would have something to do with this. He's had his greedy eyes set on this place for a good while.'

The messenger refused to say any more. 'These papers are for you, Mr Powers,' he said, handing over some pages to her father, who banged the door shut on him. 'I'll be back next month!' called the man, remounting his horse.

Eily grabbed at the pieces of paper, gasping as she read them. 'Oh my God, John! He's doubled our rent! We'll never be able to pay this much. Where does he expect us to get this kind of money?'

The paper was passed to Nano then to Michael.

'I'm sorry, Eily. I was wrong about this fella,' muttered Michael. 'I don't know what to say to ye both.'

'Maybe we could raise it,' suggested Nano. 'There's the furniture and the ornaments and ...'

Mary-Brigid watched her mother slump, weeping, in the corner near the fire.

''Tis useless! Useless!' was all she'd say. 'You can't escape your destiny!'

Mary-Brigid sat open-mouthed listening.

'You can't cheat your destiny!' Eily was ranting now. 'All of us were meant to go to the workhouse! We cheated it once, but now that's where we'll end up!' She sobbed hysterically.

'Hush, child! Hush,' begged Nano. 'We're not done for yet.'

'Eily, I promise you, we'll fight this,' said John, wrapping his arms around her. 'No-one will take this land while there's breath left in my body. I'll not have my wife and children put out on the roads.'

*   *   *

Mary-Brigid had run to hide down by the scratchy thorn bushes, for today Muck was being sold. Their half-dozen hens were already sold off, and Maisie clucked despondently around the cottage door, searching for them.

Even from a distance she could hear the pig squealing. The sound hurt her ears and heart. The Phelan brothers were buying him. 'He's a fine pig, ready for butchering,' they'd said, as Mary-Brigid had tickled

Muck's bristly head and back for the very last time.

The noise was desperate, and, by the sounds of it, the huge pig was putting up a good fight against leaving his familiar pigpen. Mary-Brigid just couldn't bear it. Eventually all the noise stopped, so, drying her eyes and blowing her nose, she collected herself and walked sadly back home.

Morning Boy whinnied to her as she passed him, as if he sensed her sadness.

'Hello, Boy!' she sighed, stopping to pat him. 'Don't be afraid, nothing's going to happen to you!' The horse gazed back at her steadily.

'Are you all right, little one?' Her uncle's voice startled her.

'Fine,' she sniffed, knowing full well that he could tell she'd been crying. But he didn't say a word about it and just stood beside her, looking at the horses.

'They like you!' he said. 'You're very good with the horses, Mary-Brigid.'

'I like them too,' she smiled. 'Uncle Michael, what happened the girl?'

'The girl?' he asked, puzzled.

'Yes, the girl you were telling me about, the one who used to own these horses?'

'Miss Felicia?' he said quietly. He thought of the young girl screaming as she'd watched her home burn to the ground. 'I told you already, pet, about the house catching fire, and how the stables were destroyed ...'

'And how you rescued Mercy and some of the others.'

'I believe Miss Felicia went back to London with her parents and her sister, Rose. They have a large house in London and Sir Henry will probably stay there. You know, in time they'll forget about Ireland and all that's happened. People do forget.'

'I'd never forget!' Mary-Brigid swore in a small voice.

'Aye,' joked Michael. 'You're a stubborn bit of a lassie, just like Peggy. Nothing will get by you.'

She gave him a watery smile.

'Come on, let's get you back up to Nano and Eily, they'll be right worried about you.'

She dragged her sleeve across her eyes and nose, drying them hastily.

'Ready, pet?'

'Aye.' She nodded.

'I promise, Mary-Brigid, I will do everything I can to help you and the family,' said Michael, taking her hand. 'We'll just have to find the money somehow.'

CHAPTER 18

Blackberry Picking

'A DAY OUT IN THE FRESH AIR blackberry picking would
do you the world of good, Eily,' Nano had suggested.
''Twould help you forget your troubles.'

The air was still and warm as Eily, Nano and
Mary-Brigid set out across the fields to go blackberry
picking. Ahead of them a tangled, winding hedgerow
of lush brambles meandered for what seemed like
miles, before the ground finally rose gently upwards
towards the slopes of the Giant's Bed.

They each carried a pail. Mary-Brigid's was the
smallest – and how she longed to fill it. Each curving
branch was laden down with the weight of huge
clusters of shiny purple-black fruit.

'I've never seen the like of it,' murmured Nano.

'Be careful of those thorns, Mary-Brigid,' advised Eily, 'and make sure to check that there are no maggots in the berries.'

Mary-Brigid nodded; she was just itching to get picking. She stuffed the first few blackberries into her mouth, relishing the strong, sweet taste, then good sense prevailed and she began to follow the example of her mother and Nano and drop them into her pail. She watched the way her mother's fingers flew along the branches. Nano picked slowly and steadily. At one stage her wide black skirt got caught up in some thorns and Mary-Brigid had to rescue her.

'What would I do without you, child?' chuckled Nano, 'I'm rightly stuck.'

It was hot, and after a while Mary-Brigid wished that she had brought a sun-bonnet as she could feel herself getting too sticky and warm. Luckily, Eily had a can of water and the three of them sat in the shade and drank from it. Mary-Brigid knew that she must look a sight with her hands and arms and chin all stained with the bright purple juice. Then Nano took a bit of a rest as the others worked on.

'Mammy, there's lashings of them, look!' Mary-Brigid pointed out, as she moved along, pushing against the trailing brambles. She picked low down as her mother stretched and picked above her, until both buckets were almost full.

'There'll be plenty of eating in this lot,' smiled Eily. 'Jams and fillings for pies and tarts and, best of all, fresh with a jug of cream. You and Daddy and Jodie will be sick of blackberries in a few weeks' time.'

'I'd never be sick of blackberries, Mammy!' declared Mary-Brigid. 'Never! But isn't it a pity you couldn't sell some of them?'

'What's that, child?' enquired Nano, rousing herself from the old tree stump that she had been sitting on.

'Well, it's only I ... I ... was sort of thinking that you and Mammy make the best jams and pies and tarts – better than anyone else – and I'm sure people might buy them ...' Mary-Brigid trailed off, feeling silly.

They were both staring at her.

'I'm sure people *would* buy them,' she continued, blushing. 'And I heard you and Daddy saying we need to get some money and I just thought that –'

'Aren't you the wise girleen!' interrupted Nano.

Eily swooped down and caught Mary-Brigid under the armpits and swung her round and round. 'Mary-Brigid Powers, you are the cleverest bit of a thing I've ever come across!'

Mary-Brigid could feel the whole world and the grass tilt beneath her when her mother stopped spinning her. Why, she was just pure dizzy with excitement!

'It will be like the old days back in the shop in Market Lane,' said Nano wistfully. 'Do you remember, Eily?'

Nano's and Eily's eyes were shining, and Mary-Brigid bounced up and down with pride beside them.

'We'll need some extra sugar and flour, Nano, and we've Maisie's eggs,' said Eily, all excited, 'and Mary-Brigid can go up to Old Drummond's place, he always used to let the children pick some apples when he was alive. Folks always like a nice blackberry and apple pie.'

'Jams and chutneys and pies ...' Nano was busy planning too. 'Eily, you could go door-to-door selling, but to my mind the market is the best place for home produce.'

'What do you think John will say to all this?' asked Eily.

'He'll say what a good wife you are, pet, and what a smart daughter he's got. That's what he'll say.'

At long last, despite all the chat and excitement, all three pails were full.

'And we can come back again and again, and there'll still be plenty more,' said Eily happily.

Mary-Brigid could just about manage to lift her pail, and she had to walk carefully so as not to spill any of the precious berries. Her mother strode ahead of her, humming softly under her breath. It seemed such a long time since she'd heard her mother laugh or sing. The sound did her heart good.

CHAPTER 19

Market Day

OVER THE NEXT FEW DAYS, Eily and Nano worked long
and hard in the little kitchen, washing and preparing
the fruit. Miley Lynch, from the small public bar near
the school, had let them help themselves to a pile of
empty jars and bottles in his yard, and they had washed
them out then boiled them in water till they were
spotlessly clean. Every pot and pan in the place was in
use as they boiled fruit and sugar. The smell of sweet
syrup and apples filled the cottage.

Naturally, young Jodie was full of curiosity, and
screamed when he was pulled away from hot things
for fear he'd burn himself.

'Mary-Brigid, the best thing you can do to help us is
to take your little brother out of the way,' suggested

Eily, so the children were forced to watch the goings-on from the doorway.

Nano spread a dusting of flour on the table and rolled out pale, oaten-coloured dough to make the pies. Then she quickly pared and sliced the apples and popped them in on top of the pastry.

They filled each glass jar with sweet jam and crab-apple and bramble jelly, and bottled the preserves and richly coloured chutneys.

Nano cut circles out of left-over scraps of cloth from the work-basket to tie on the lids, and Eily sat up till late in the night inscribing labels of white paper, which they glued on, saying: HOMEMADE BLACKBERRY JAM.

Michael sat in the corner watching them work. 'This is just like being back at Nano and Lena's,' he said happily.

Eventually everything was finished, and Eily placed the jars and wide-necked bottles carefully in two huge straw baskets, ready for the morning. Nano had agreed to stay at home to mind Jodie. Michael would stay too, to mind the horses and help Nano if she needed it. Mary-Brigid and John and Eily would go to the market bright and early.

The Phelan brothers had lent John their donkey and cart and he had already loaded a creel of turf up onto the back. The baskets were put firmly in position, while

Eily and Mary-Brigid held about a dozen pies between them on the seat, along with a tray of Nano's oat-and-apple biscuits, trying to keep the whole lot from falling as they slowly jogged along.

The Saturday-morning market was held in the centre off Castletaggart, and by the time they arrived many of the stall-holders had already set up. John took down two long *sugán* rope stools he had brought, and they balanced the baskets on one of them and the pies on the other.

For their first hour not a soul bought anything. All the passers-by were people just like themselves, anxious to sell something, hoping to make their rent money. Mary-Brigid watched anxiously as a procession of countryfolk, with geese and hens and ducks, filed by. Men carried big rounds of hard yellow cheese, and there were stalls with long pats of golden butter, stamped with circles of curving flowers. Clothes and clocks and household hardware and white-and-blue crockery – no matter what a person wanted, they could buy it at the Saturday market.

Then Eily decided that they should perhaps move to a better position, so Mary-Brigid helped to drag their things across to the other side of the wide green.

In what seemed like the blink of an eye the pies and biscuits were all sold out!

'Nano will be right pleased,' laughed Eily, patting the pocket of her skirt and listening to the reassuring jingle of coins. But they still hadn't sold any jam.

Mary-Brigid watched the stall across from them, where a mother and daughter were busy selling all sorts of bread and huge meat-pies and puddings. Judging by their conversation, many of the customers were regulars. They both watched enviously as customer after customer bought.

'Mammy! They'd buy our jam if they only knew how good it tasted,' said Mary-Brigid, trying to console her mother. 'Maybe I could open a pot or two?'

'Listen, pet,' suggested Eily, 'run across to the stall over yonder and buy a cake of soda bread. Here's the money! And ask the lady if by any chance she could lend us a knife.'

The woman looked puzzled but obliged them, and Mary-Brigid ran back with a floury, golden cake of soda-bread. Straight away Eily began to slice it and lay it on an empty biscuit tray. She plopped a lump of rich blackberry jam on each small piece of bread.

'Now, Mary-Brigid, these are for our customers!' she announced, and she stood in front of the baskets and offered the slices to any passerby who looked like they might be customers. One jolly-looking woman bought three pots of jam while she stood munching on the bread. A gentleman stopped to buy some relish and several pots of Nano's thick chutney.

Soon a sizeable group of curious people had gathered to sample their produce and to buy. Eily pointed some of them in the direction of the woman who had made the bread, and the woman waved cheerily over to them.

Finally one basket was totally empty and the other held only two pots of jam and a jar of chutney.

Mary-Brigid noticed that many of the stall-holders were packing up and putting their things away as the market came to an end.

The girl from the stall across from them appeared at their stall. 'My Mammy said to give you this and to thank you for the extra custom you sent us.' She handed Mary-Brigid a huge meat-pie. One piece of crust had broken slightly, but heated up it would make a grand meal.

'Thank you,' said Eily, 'and please take a pot of jam from us.'

The young girl grinned. 'Will ye be back in two weeks?' she asked. 'We usually come every second week.'

Mary-Brigid watched anxiously as her mother thought about it. They could definitely make more jams and preserves and Nano seemed to know the kind of confectionery people wanted to buy.

'Aye,' Eily replied, 'we'll be back.'

'Well, see you then,' and the girl grinned at Mary-Brigid before running back to join her mother.

Mary-Brigid helped to lift the empty baskets as they went to meet John. He was standing in the distance, the cart empty, all the turf sold. 'A widow woman who lives on her own in the middle of the town took the lot,' he explained, 'and she wants me to deliver to her every few weeks.'

'Oh that's grand, John,' said Eily. 'We've all done really well by the looks of it.'

'Daddy, there's a meat pie for the tea too,' Mary-Brigid told him.

'I'm proud of ye both,' he said, as they climbed up on the cart.

'We know,' beamed Mary-Brigid. 'Come on, let's get away home quick and tell the others the good news.'

CHAPTER 20

The Decision

PEGGY MASHED THE POTATOES, almost pulverising them. Mrs O'Connor arched her eyebrows in surprise. She watched as the young maid walloped them down into the warming bowl.

Two days ago she had said goodbye to Sarah in a hurry, standing outside the side-door of the factory. Both of them were in tears as they hugged each other. It might be years before they'd see each other again, if ever.

Sarah had promised to write and let her know of all her adventures. James and John had already purchased a wagon and a pair of fine strong horses, and they were now busy gathering supplies for the journey ahead.

Peggy just couldn't imagine life in Boston without

Sarah and John and James. Who would she visit when they were gone? Who would she tell stories of Mrs O'Connor and the Rowans to? Who would she spend her days off with? Who would she twirl and dance around the room with at the next *céilí* if James was not there?

She pushed a piece of hair out of her eyes with her sleeve, trying not to sniff.

Mrs O'Connor's attention was drawn to a movement down on the pathway. It was a tall young man, striding towards the kitchen door.

'Peggy!' called the cook. 'There's a visitor at the door!'

Peggy looked up from her work, and, wiping her hands on her apron, went to the door. There was no one there. Then she spotted him standing under the wide cherry tree waiting for her. It was James.

Her heart skipped a beat as she ran towards him. Maybe Sarah was sick or something? She could tell he was nervous.

'Peggy, I couldn't go without saying goodbye to you properly,' he said as soon as she reached him.

'Oh!' Peggy didn't know how to respond.

'We're leaving first thing in the morning and I just had to see you, one last time.'

She bit her lip hard, trying to stop the tears.

'I made a mess of it the last time we met,' he

continued, shyly. 'It sounded like I didn't care that much whether you came with us ... but I do care ... I ... I love you very much, Peggy. I've loved you practically from the first day I met you on the *Fortunata*.'

Peggy stared at him. He had lost his nervousness now, and looked earnest.

He spoke urgently. 'I waited and waited, Peggy, to give you time to grow up. Perhaps I waited too long.'

Peggy blushed, looking down at her apron.

'John and I always planned to work a few years in the east before heading out to the new frontier. But you had always been part of my plan, Peggy. It's your face I want to see first thing in the morning and last thing at night. That's why I asked you to be my wife.'

Peggy put her face in her hands, trying to compose herself.

He touched her hair gently. 'I wanted you to know that before I left. Goodbye, Peggy, my love!'

Peggy raised her head. He was looking at her so sadly it almost broke her heart.

'James!' she screamed like a wild-cat, flinging herself at him, pulling his face down to meet hers. 'Don't you dare go without me!' she said in between the warmth of his kisses.

Then, holding her skirt and apron, she flew back up the path, pushed in the kitchen door, much to the surprise of Mrs O'Connor and the housekeeper, and chased up the back stairs. Out of breath and panting, she kicked open the door of her room.

She grabbed her battered hold-all and started to pull stockings and underwear from the makeshift line she and Kitty had strung from the beams. She added her two good blouses and fine wool skirt and the lavender-coloured floral print dress she had saved for and bought last year. Her two nightdresses – one dirty, one clean – her flannel, cologne and a bar of scented soap. From the hook behind the door she took her warm winter coat, and her stout black brogues from under the bed. She retrieved her bank book, along with some letters from under the mattress, a few books, and finally her family bible, where Nano had written the names on her family tree. Soon there would be another name added to it when Peggy O'Driscoll married James Connolly. She ran her finger excitedly along the page of writing.

She stopped and stared. The room seemed suddenly empty, the two brass beds deserted. Fingering the horse-hair bracelet that Michael had made for her when she was leaving home for America, Peggy remembered the good times here with Kitty, but now she knew there would be good times ahead too. With a sigh, she pulled the door closed after her, frightened that James would be gone or that she had imagined it all.

He was not. He was sitting in the kitchen with the cook and the housekeeper who were chatting away to him like old friends.

Perhaps Miss Whitman would insist on her working her proper notice or object to her leaving like this? Peggy felt scared as she stood in the kitchen and lowered her bag to the floor.

'Miss Whitman, I'm sorry about my notice, but I ... I have to go ... now,' she said firmly, her eyes meeting those of her future husband.

Miss Whitman did not seem too put out. 'There's a lot to be said for the rules of the heart! You don't want to end up like me, Peggy lass.'

'Will you explain to Mrs Rowan about me leaving?' Peggy said. 'She's been so kind to me over the years and I hate letting her down.'

Mrs O'Connor was blowing her nose loudly. 'Oh Peggy, dear! I'll truly miss you. What will I do without your big brown eyes listening to my stories and cheering me up?'

Peggy hugged the motherly cook. 'You'll tell Kitty what happened, won't you? And send me her address when I'm settled? I'll write to you all. I promise.'

'Of course!' Mrs O'Connor agreed. 'Now, I've told your young man that Father Vincent does the early mass in Saint Patrick's – he married my daughter, you know. He'll look after you.'

'Oh thank you, Mrs O'Connor,' beamed Peggy. 'Sarah can be my bridesmaid –'

'Peggy, what will I do about your wages?' broke in Miss Whitman. 'There's at least a month due and Mr Rowan had intended a special bonus for all the help with the wedding.'

Peggy considered. She had her bank book. There would be money there to purchase lumber and horse-feed, and curtains and blankets – all the things herself and James might need. Now that she would have a home of her own to build, Eily would miss the small twice-a-year gifts she sent her.

'I'm not sure where I'll be next month or the month after,' she said. 'I'll tell you what, Miss Whitman, would you ever be so kind as to send it to my sister, Eily, back home in Ireland? Here, I'll scribble the address for you. Tell her it's a present from me.'

Hugging them both and laughing with pleasure, Peggy O'Driscoll said her last farewells to Rushton. Then she and James sat arm-in-arm in the cart as they drove away from the house.

CHAPTER 21

The Rent Collector

THE GINGER-HAIRED MAN with the bristly bit of a moustache came back, just as he had promised.

Every night for the last week, Eily and John had emptied out the small earthenware jar they kept hidden under the bed and counted out their money. They had got a fine price for Muck and the hen-money added some more; then there was all they'd made on two visits to the market. Still, no matter how they added it up, they were short the amount due. Mary-Brigid wished for a miracle that would change the copper coins into silver or gold.

'Come inside, Mr Brennan,' said John. 'We have the money for you.'

They all watched anxiously as the man counted out the money into the palm of his hand.

'Mr Powers, there seems to be some sort of misunderstanding. This amount falls short of the terms agreed.'

John's wide hands gripped the table. 'There's no mistake, Mr Brennan. That's all there is. I've nothing left to sell. My rent is double what it was this time last year. It's all I'm able to pay. You'll have to tell that to Mr Ormonde!'

Mr Brennan seemed embarrassed. He looked around the cottage, taking in the young husband and wife with their two small children, and the old lady in the corner who glared fiercely at him. He hated this job of rent-collecting for Hussey.

'I'll talk to them, Mr Powers. Are ye sure you've nothing else to give me?' he prodded.

'No!' said John firmly. 'There's only the food on the children's plates and the clothes on their backs. Tell Dennis Ormonde that I have worked as hard as any man can work — and that's all I have!'

Mary-Brigid watched as Mr Brennan scooped their money into a leather bag. 'I'll talk to Mr Hussey on your behalf,' promised the man, now anxious to leave. They all watched as he hoisted himself onto the saddle of his sturdy grey mare and rode away.

'Now we wait!' said John seriously.

CHAPTER 22

Siege

THEY WAITED AND WAITED – and they made their plans. Mary-Brigid helped her father to fill a huge sack with potatoes, which he and Michael dragged into the cottage. Every spare pot and pail and jar was filled with water from the well and put to stand in the coolest part of the kitchen, and no clothes were left on the washing line. John's work-tools were brought in from the small outhouse, and now his spade, pitchfork, scythe and hoe stood against the kitchen wall. Maisie, too, was brought in, and she spent her time clucking angrily at Scrap, who was none too pleased with the visitor. Nano and Eily checked the flour and oatmeal barrels, and Michael and John dragged the huge kitchen dresser, which Mary-Brigid's grandfather had made, over beside the door.

'Mary-Brigid, you are to keep an eye on your little brother. You must not go more than a few yards from the house. Do you understand me?' ordered her father.

'Aye,' she said, fearful of what was going on.

That night she slept fitfully, and in the morning found that Michael's settle bed near the fire had not been slept on.

'Michael's gone!' She ran to her parents with the news.

'This isn't his fight,' said Nano. 'And he has things to see to ...'

Mary-Brigid looked out the cottage door. 'The horses are gone too!' she announced.

At midday Mary-Brigid's heart leapt when she heard the sound of horses' hooves in the laneway. She stared down the boreen; it was Mr Brennan and four other men.

'Inside, Mary-Brigid,' ordered John sharply. 'Stand back from the window.'

He bent down and put his shoulder against the dresser. Then he and Nano and Eily strained to shove the heavy weight against the door.

After a few minutes a voice called out: 'Mr Powers, it's me, Tom Brennan. I'm afraid the amount you paid is unacceptable. Your landlord is insisting on the correct amount.'

'I told you, I don't have it!' shouted John.

Another voice spoke. 'By the order of the landlord Dennis Ormonde, you, John Powers, and your dependants are asked to quit this holding.'

''Tis Hussey!' said John.

William Hussey sat astride his large, chestnut horse. One side of his severe-looking face seemed almost crooked, the skin puckered and scarred. His left arm hung uselessly at his side.

'I'll not quit!' yelled John. 'Tell Ormonde I'll give up the low field if that will reduce the rent.'

Low voices spoke outside, as if arguing. Then Mr Hussey rode closer to the door. 'This land will not be divided up,' he announced. 'There's no arguing. You either pay the full rate for this holding or you give it up. Mr Ormonde is a very busy man. He leaves the running of the estate to me.'

'You just want this farm for yourself, Hussey! You'll not get it!' shouted John.

'How dare you!' The landlord's agent cursed. 'You've not heard the end of this! Not by a long chalk.'

Two men were left guarding the cottage while the others rode off. John hoped that Mr Brennan was honest enough to tell the landlord of his offer.

Night-time fell and the family hardly slept. Eily sat in a chair by the small window, keeping watch lest Hussey and his men came back.

In the morning the cawing of the rooks from the nearby woods woke them. Bleary-eyed, Mary-Brigid had a sip of milk and a chunk of bread. Her father looked exhausted, but took over the watch. Eily dressed and washed Jodie and tried to amuse him. Nano finally roused herself, her old bones weary from it all.

William Hussey and his men returned, and they seemed to be pulling something. It was like a tree trunk, and they came to a halt with it just outside the door.

'John Powers! Do you agree to pay the rent set by your landlord Dennis Ormonde?' Mr Hussey said clearly.

'I have given you almost double my previous rent,' answered John in desperation. 'I haven't one brass farthing more. I have even offered to give up one of my fields to make up the shortfall.'

'You have refused to pay the full rent!' jeered Mr Hussey.

'I have been a good tenant, just like my father and grandfather before me. I have no fight with Mr Ormonde. He knows that I've paid more than a fair rent,' shouted John.

Mr Hussey turned his horse around. 'We give you an hour to pack up your belongings and leave this dwelling,' he declared.

Inside the small cottage they all stood bewildered and shocked, not knowing what to do. Jodie began to cry and clung to his father, who hoisted him up in his arms. Nano began to move around, folding things, putting them in small bundles.

'What are you doing, Nano?' said Eily.

'I'm beginning to pack up,' said Nano quietly, trying to hide the despair in her voice.

'We are not packing up, Nano!' said John firmly. 'Sit down. All of ye sit down!'

From his face and manner, Nano knew that this was one time to respect the young man's wishes.

Mary-Brigid felt so nervous that she could hear her own heart beating in her chest. Eily stood, looking helpless and as pale as a ghost. They all sat waiting.

After an hour one of the men took a huge pitchfork and began to pull the straw from the thatched roof. The others moved the tree-trunk closer to the house. Mary-Brigid closed her eyes, waiting for the thud as it hit against their wooden door.

'Now!' called William Hussey.

The men gave a huge push and the small cottage seemed to shudder as the ramming tree-trunk battered against the door, but the heavy old oak dresser took the brunt of the impact.

'Again!' ordered Mr Hussey.

The family braced themselves for another thud, and within the space of a few minutes their home was hit again, and again. The door split and it was obvious that the dresser could not hold for much longer. There was a gaping hole in the roof too, through which they could see the sky. Then someone blocked the chimney in an effort to smoke them out. Stinging tears ran down their faces, and the smoke made them cough and choke.

Mary-Brigid guessed that they would have to leave soon. Poor Jodie was choking so badly he could scarcely get his breath. Barely moving, Eily held the child tightly to her, standing as if she had been turned into stone.

'Mr Hussey! Mr Hussey!'

They all heard the shouts. It was Michael's voice. Michael had come back.

'Stop that! Stop those men!' he yelled, as he ran towards the cottage. 'Leave them be!'

William Hussey turned to face him. 'Who the hell are you? What business of this is yours?'

'Eily is my sister and this is her home.'

'Her home, indeed!' jeered the land-agent.

'Mr Hussey! What do you think is the value of this holding and the cottage? How much would it cost to buy?' questioned Michael, standing with his hands in his waistcoat pocket.

'Buy! Sure, they can't even afford to pay the proper rent!' guffawed the ruddy-faced man. 'This farm would cost them at least forty pounds to purchase.'

'Forty pounds!' repeated Michael. 'That's what you're telling me this place would cost.'

'Yes,' nodded Mr Hussey, glaring around at the few neighbours who had arrived and were now standing down by the gateway, watching.

''Tis done!' shouted Michael, looking him square in the face, and catching a hold of the leather bridle of his horse.

'What do you mean, done?'

'I'm telling you the truth,' said Michael. 'Check with Mr Ormonde. The eviction order has been cancelled, and this land has been sold.' A gasp went up from the neighbours. 'Now, I'd advise you to stop those men, Mr Hussey, otherwise you'll have to pay a large amount for the damage you're doing!'

'Where's you proof?' shouted Mr Hussey.

'My proof is with Mr Ormonde. You can check it for yourself,' said Michael.

Hussey jerked at the reins, turning his horse. 'You little whipper-snapper, I'll take my crop to you with your lies and falsehoods! I'll find out what's going on. You haven't heard the last of me. I'll be back and I'll have the constable with me to arrest ye all and throw you off this property!'

'They are no longer tenants!' said Michael icily. 'You can do nothing.'

William Hussey and his men abandoned the battering ram and made their way across the fields, leaving the cottage standing, the frightened family staring out after them.

CHAPTER 23

Glengarry

'IS IT TRUE?' Eily stood in front of her brother, while the youngsters hugged and kissed him.

'Aye, 'tis true,' he said softly. 'This house and the land that goes with it now belong to you and all your descendants, Eily.'

'Michael, what in heaven's name did you do?'

'I sold Glengarry. She's a fine mare. She's won some of the best races in her day and has bred a few winners already.'

'I can't believe it,' cried Eily, tears running down her face. 'You sold your horse! But you had such plans for Glengarry.'

'I reckoned Mr Ormonde was the kind of man who liked to have a bit of a bet. Turns out he knows Sir

Henry Buckland and had heard of Castletaggart stables. He's a good judge of horse flesh, I'll give him that, and he only had to take one look at the mare and he wanted her. He's hoping to build up his stables. He doesn't care about farming, he reckons racing's the thing! Glengarry won't let him down. She's a good breeding mare.'

'A horse is worth that much?' said Eily, amazed.

'A valuable racehorse is,' said Michael. 'And racing is all that matters to a gambling man like Mr Ormonde.'

'Well! I still can't believe it.'

'I did promise him that I'd give him a bit of advice on getting that shambles of a stables he has into some kind of shape – to be run along the lines of my old place.'

'Did you indeed!' Eily half-smiled.

'Eily, don't forget there was also all that money you and John gave to Mr Brennan.'

'You did all this for us, Michael!' she said, overcome.

'Eily, you're my family. 'Tis the very least I could do,' he said proudly, his dark eyes shining. 'Anyway, 'tis all signed and sealed now, the holding is in your names.'

'Come here, child! Let me give you a hug,' called Nano, who was sitting, still very shaken, over by the fireside. Michael smiled to himself as his elderly aunt squeezed him tightly, and pushed his thick curls back off his face, just the way she used to do when he was a young boy. 'Michael, your parents would have been right proud of you,' she said, her voice filled with emotion, 'and I'm right proud of you – of ye all!' she added firmly.

CHAPTER 24

Wagons West

PEGGY TOUCHED THE NARROW BAND OF GOLD that circled her finger. Married! She still couldn't believe that James was her husband. Mrs James Connolly! It sounded grand.

She squeezed his hand as they sat side-by-side on the front seat of their wagon, and jogged along the worn, dusty trail through yet another field. Vivid blue cornflowers stretched skywards in the heat. Peggy was mighty glad of the simple white sun bonnet that protected her eyes from the glare. Already she could feel a warm line tracing a fresh batch of freckles across her nose and cheeks.

James and herself had been wed five days ago. Father O'Hara had married them in a simple ceremony after the twelve o'clock mass in the small parish church of St Patrick's. John had given her away, and Sarah had been her bridesmaid. Peggy had worn a light lavender-blue dress, and Sarah had lent her a new cream satin bonnet which she had dressed with sprays of flowers.

Oh how she wished that Eily and Nano and Michael had been there to share it all with her! Instead, Mrs O'Connor had appeared and made a big fuss over her. She gave her a present of a grandmother clock.

'It's far too much!' said Peggy, but Mrs O' Connor had insisted.

'You have to have something to remember Rushton by, and all your years working in Greenbay.' The grandmother clock had stood on the mantelpiece in Mrs O'Connor's bedroom. Peggy knew that once she got settled, she would find a special place for it.

Afterwards they had a fine meal which Sarah had prepared, and Mrs O'Connor and Father O'Hara joined them. It was all very different from the lavish wedding party that Miss Roxanne had enjoyed, but looking around her at the table and seeing the love and affection in James's eyes, and knowing that Sarah, her best friend was now her sister, Peggy's happiness was complete.

Going west! They were on their way. Sarah and John's wagon was up ahead of them. They had joined the wagon-train last Wednesday, and Peggy had stepped up into her very first home, a canvas-covered wagon, with a roll-down mattress bed, a side-bench to sit on and a simple, low table. One half was given over to provisions for the journey and for their new life and homestead.

There were two other Irish families on the wagon train, the O'Hallorans and the Callaghans. Many of their fellow travellers were Dutch, and already she had met Ben Maasen, with his twinkling eyes, who had teased her about being a new bride. 'You come and talk to my missus. She knows all there is to know about being married!' he offered. Arlene, his wife, had smiled warmly at her, and introduced their four flaxen-haired children.

Peggy tried to put stories she had heard about Indians and stampedes of buffalo and wild mountain cats and grizzly bears out of her head. Adam Shelton, the wagon-train leader, seemed a good and sensible man who would guide them well on their journey.

Sometimes it seemed to Peggy that her whole life, well, all the important pieces of it, seemed to involve a journey of some sort or other. There was the journey when she was only a little girl, about the same age as Ben Maasen's daughter, when she had walked until every bone in her body ached and her feet bled and the hunger pains in her stomach had all but driven her crazy in the midst of a starving people, holding onto her big sister's hand. Then there was that awful voyage from Ireland on the *Fortunata*, the ship on which she had first met Sarah and John and her beloved James. She shut her eyes, remembering it all.

'Are you all right, Peggy?' asked James, his voice full of concern, as he held the leather reins and guided the two horses.

'I'm fine,' she smiled. 'Just fine.' She leaned over and kissed his cheek. 'James, I was thinking, the first town we come to, I must post this letter to my family back home. I want them to know all about you, and the wedding and how happy I am.'

He turned to her and smiled lovingly.

Ahead of them lay miles and miles of unexplored territory. It was a long road and a hard journey ahead, but that didn't bother Peggy a bit, now that she had James beside her. She was on a wagon train, going near half-way across America, just imagine! But this was one journey she really wanted to make.

CHAPTER 25

A Sod of Earth

MARY-BRIGID STOOD IN THE CENTRE of their cottage. The wooden door lay smashed to smithereens and the dresser was cracked. Through the hole in the roof she could see the evening sky, where the first star was appearing. All their furniture lay in a heap together. Two panes of glass in the window were broken.

'Tomorrow we'll start to fix the place,' assured her father.

She followed the rest of them outside. Nano was leaning on Michael's arm and John carried Jodie on his shoulders. It was almost dark and the scraggy shadows of thorn bushes and furze danced wildly. The fields and low stone walls lay spread out, dark and mysterious, around them. In the distance she heard the soft whinny of a horse – a young horse.

'Morning Boy! Will ye stop that or I'll have Ormonde down here wanting to buy you too!' laughed Michael.

'I was afraid you'd sold him,' murmured Mary-Brigid.

'What makes you think I'd be so foolish as to sell one of the best racehorses Ireland's ever likely to see?' joked Michael. ''Tis going to be a lot of work looking after him, Mary-Brigid, now that his foster mother's gone. And seeing I'll be busy I'll be needing some sort of a helper.'

'Me, you mean?' asked Mary-Brigid, her eyes sparkling.

Michael smiled at her delight.

'Mary-Brigid, come over here to me,' called Eily gently. 'Look around you, Mary-Brigid.' Her mother bent down and lifted up a heavy sod of earth. 'Open your hands, pet.'

Eily placed the sod in Mary-Brigid's open hands. The earth felt hard and heavy and damp. It smelt of peat and new grass and all the things that had grown in it for hundreds and hundreds of years.

'Hold this sod, Mary-Brigid, and remember this day and this night! This is the day that these fields and this land and this hard-worked soil finally became ours!'

Mary-Brigid stood under the dark, spreading sky, and vowed never to forget.